That's Why I Love You

Angel DeVille

Published by Angel DeVille, 2024.

This is a work of fiction. Similarities to real people, places, or events are entirely coincidental.

THAT'S WHY I LOVE YOU

First edition. August 20, 2024.

Copyright © 2024 Angel DeVille.

ISBN: 979-8227431233

Written by Angel DeVille.

Table of Contents

Prologue

I saw him across the room. He looked up and saw me too. I blushed. He smiled.

There was an instant attraction between us. I could feel the sexual energy in the air.

I had been watching him since I arrived.

Do I want to get involved with him?

I don't know but damn, he looked good. He intrigued me.

We had been giving each other some strong sexual vibes from across the room. Just the thought of a secret encounter made me curious.

Our eyes met, yet only for a moment. He looked like he could devour me instantly.

As I took a sip of my drink, I saw him leave the room.

My stomach sank. A tinge of disappointment ran across me.

Did he just leave? Is he gone for good?

I looked around to see if I could just catch a glimpse of him, somewhere - *anywhere.*

I felt as if he was still watching me. Watching me frantically look for him. I could still feel his gaze.

I decided to excuse myself to the kitchen to try and see where he may have ventured.

As I approached the kitchen, he snatched me into the bedroom across the hall from the kitchen.

He quickly closes the door and locks it.

"I've been watching you all night." He says.

"Really?"

"Yes." He said.

The sexual tension was present in the room. He grabbed me and kissed me hard, his tongue probing my mouth. *So much for introductions.*

Chapter 1 - Meet

SIEDAH

. . . .

"GIRL, ARE YOU REALLY coming tonight? I mean 'cuz I've been asking yo' ass and well, we both know how it ends." Monica said sarcastically over the phone.

I could imagine her face - her head tilted to the side, rolling her eyes and her lips pursed up like she doesn't believe a damn word that's coming out my mouth.

"Yes bitch, I'm coming."

"Yeah bitch, I've heard that shit before." She said as I heard her blow out smoke.

"Bitch, ain't you at work?" I asked as I looked at the clock. I was ready to get my ass off and out of the building for real. It was Friday and I needed to change up this weekend.

. . . .

"YEAH, AND?" SHE SAID. "It's just a vape, I ain't stupid Siedah."

"Shit, I can't do nothing at the job." I looked around at the almost empty office.

"Well, I'm about to get off soon so, I'll see you later for real?" I could hear the doubt in her voice.

"Yes! I'm coming! For Real! Damn," I said, raising my voice. I looked around hoping anyone that was still in the office would just mind their own fucking business.

"A'ight Siedah. I'll see you there then. You know where it is right?"

"Yeah, but send me the address again so I can put it on Google maps." I said, searching for my phone in my purse.

"A'ight, see you later." Monica said, hanging up the phone. I'm sure she still didn't believe me that I was gonna come through. I'll just have to prove her ass wrong.

• • • •

MONICA AND I GO WAY back. We grew up in the same neighborhood in the Chatham area of Chicago. We still kick it sometimes like back in the day, we just moved around the city. Monica wanted me to come to her boyfriend's place because he's having a house party. He's a music producer and he has a few of his music buddies coming over for networking purposes. From what I hear, he is supposed to be working with a few up-and-coming artists that show a lot of potential.

I'm just going because I want to get my drink on. I really don't care about showing my face to be honest. I'm only doing it to support Monica, who in turn is supporting her man, Franklin.

Monica was not happy that I dragged my ass to the party and arrived by the time the party was in full swing. Shit, she should have been happy my ass made it at all, but she wasn't.

"It took yo' ass long enough." She said, handing me a Corona as I walked through the door. I looked around and there were a bunch of people - *everywhere.* This was why I should've stayed at home. I didn't feel like rubbing elbows with anyone.

"Bitch you betta be happy I showed the fuck up." I said taking a swig of my drink.

"I am happy you showed up, I just wanted to introduce you to someone." She said looking around.

"See, this is why I shouldn't have come." I turned around and headed for the door.

Monica always tries to set me up with one of Franklin's buddies or someone that she knows.

"Girl, wait! A'ight." She begged as she grabbed my arm.

"Why you always do this? See, this is why I never come out and hang with you."

"I'm sorry," she said, looking sincere. "I just want you to meet him. You ain't gotta marry him, just meet."

"No, why I gotta meet someone? Did you tell him I wasn't interested in any kind of relationship with anyone?"

"Naw." She said looking slyly.

"What?"

"I didn't tell him that I wanted to introduce him to someone."

"What the fuck Monica?" I said, raising my voice.

"Shhhh, bitch. I said I was sorry." She said, grabbing my arm and dragging me back to the bedroom.

"What the fuck?"

"He's pretty much your twin."

"Again, what the fuck? What do you mean my twin?"

"He's a friend of Franklin's. He had a really bad break up back in the day and he doesn't date."

"And you trying to set me up with him?" I asked, trying to make sense of it all.

"Yeah. Naw. Well…" Monica sang.

"Which one is it Monica?" I said getting irritated. I turned the Corona upside down, taking the rest of the beer down in just a few gulps.

"Well, it's like this," she said as she walked over to the dresser and picked up a blunt and lit it. "He ain't tryin to get with anyone either, but he's trying to 'kick it' with someone, if you know what I mean?"

"Naw bitch, I don't know what you mean." I was getting tired of this shit with her.

"Bitch, you know what I mean - *fuck buddies*." She blurted out as she passed the blunt to me.

"Oh," I said, sounding interested. "I see. Now yo' ass is pimping me out?"

"What the fuck?"

"Just fucking with you. What does he look like?"

"Well he is a good looking brother with dreads. Nice body, a bit on the athletic side" Monica said trying to describe him.

"Bitch, that's about half the niggas up in this place." I puffed on the blunt again before passing it back.

"I know, shit. That didn't help. Well if yo' ass would have come a bit earlier, you probably would have met him. I don't even know if he is still here or not." She said, heading for the door and opening it.

"Well when you find him, let me know and I'll make my own fucking decision." I said blowing out the smoke and raising my eyebrows..

"Thank you bitch. I knew you loved me," Monica smiled as she walked out the room.

"Yeah yeah, I don't know why I let you put me through this." I quipped following behind her.

"Bitch, I told you 'cuz you love me." She grinned in my face.

"Yes, I do love yo' crazy ass." I shook my head smiling at her.

"Yo, Monica!" I heard Franklin yelling her name from somewhere in the party.

"Hey, I'll be back," she said while passing the blunt to me. "Here hit that and I'll be back."

"Bitch, just so you know, if you take too long - this bitch will be gone!" I said pointing at the blunt. Monica didn't even turn around; she just gave me the thumbs up and kept walking into the crowd until she disappeared from my sight.

I walked around smoking on the blunt; Franklin had a lot of motherfuckers up in the place. There were wall to wall niggas and females all over the place. The aroma of marijuana filled the air as I puffed along while making my way back to the front of the place.

Someone caught my eye as I glided past a few people. He was talking to Franklin and a few other people. Monica was filling up the drinks around the group, keeping the party going. He looked up and caught my eye. We stared at each other for a moment and heat started to build. There was an instant attraction to him. My vajayjay started quivering as if she saw what this motherfucker looked like.

• • • •

I CROSSED THE ROOM to avoid giving him the idea to approach me. I picked up another beer from the cooler and kept walking. As I was trying to fade into the background, another person had their eye on me.

"Hello beautiful." I heard a voice say. I turned around and it's a nice looking brotha, with dreadlocks smiling at me and holding a drink - by the smell of it - *it was Hennesey*.

"Hello." I said, turning back around and looking for another place to hide out.

"I've never seen you before at one of Frank's parties. Are you a dancer?" He asked. *How cliche.* Of course a fine, beautiful black woman would *have to be* a dancer in a video in order to be at a music producer's party, right?

"No, I'm not. I'm an editor." I said, entertaining him with an answer. He was surprised by my reply and stepped back while looking me up and down.

"Really? An editor? Like a magazine?" He wasn't expecting me to have a real job.

"No, like a book. A novel."

"Oh." He sang, looking as if he had never picked up a book to read.

"Excuse me, I need to.... go over there." I said, just pointing randomly and leaving.

"Oh ok." I heard him say as I walked away.

I made my way to the other side of the room, which was rather large to say the least. Franklin had a very nice house, one could tell he was doing *well* in the music business. I saw Monica looking around as if she was looking for me; which was my queue to move around.

As I found a corner to plant myself in, I slowly surveyed the room when I caught sight of the sexy guy from earlier staring back at me. It took me by surprise when our eyes locked.

He smiled. My stomach dropped. He had been watching me from afar.

How long had he been watching me? He was fine as fuck and it's been a minute since a sistah got some.

I tried to slide out of focus as I saw him move from his location.

Was he coming over to me? My pulse increased. *What the fuck is happening?*

When I looked again, he laughed at me and I couldn't do anything but smile. It was like playing a game of cat and mouse. The attraction was there and we both knew how to play it well. He looked fuckable for sure and if I could, I would - hit it right here in this motherfucking house. In secret of course. It's way too many niggas up in here to let anyone know anything. This wasn't gonna turn into an orgy.

I looked up and took a sip of my beer as I saw him leave the room. *Was he leaving so soon?*

I didn't even get a chance to find out who he was. It's okay, but honestly I was a little disappointed. I would have given him a nice ride. I started looking around to see if I could catch just a glimpse of him somewhere - *anywhere.*

A chill went across my back. I felt as though I was being watched.

But from where? By whom? He had to be still watching me, looking frantically all over the place just trying to find him.

I decided to head back towards the kitchen to see if he headed in that direction. As I walked down the hallway to the kitchen, a door opened up and someone pulled me inside and closed the door!

To my surprise, it was the sexy brotha from earlier. I stared at him as he locked the door behind us.

"I've been watching you all night." He said.

"Really?"

"Yes."

The sexual tension was present in the room.

He grabbed me and kissed me hard, his tongue probing my mouth.

So much for introductions.

Chapter 2 - Condom

SIEDAH

· · · ·

"MMMMM...," I MOANED as he kissed my neck and down across my collarbone.

Music was blaring on the other side of the room and *this was happening*.

I wish I could slow down the time as I grabbed the sides of his shirt pulling him closer. I could feel his dick through his pants. He grabbed both of my ass cheeks at the same time while he bit my neck sending chills down my spine.

Yup, this was happening!

I backed up to the edge of the bed, pulling him with me.

He stopped and looked at me. He was sexy as hell. His black dreads hung down, freshly retwisted. Thick, juicy lips that look like he could suck the shit out of some pussy.

He licked his lips and my panties instantly got wet.

He leaned in and licked my lips as I gazed directly in his eyes.

I grabbed the bottom of his shirt and pulled it up over his head, exposing his pumped chest with tattoos plastered on both pecs and across his torso. His body smelled like Calvin Klein as his pants hung low enough to show just the right part of his pelvis that I liked to lick.

I lost my breath. I felt his hot breath against my skin as he licked down to my chest.

Just enough moonlight entered the room which allowed us to see each other's silhouette.

He slowly untied my halter romper dress from around my neck; it dropped exposing my twins and my high waisted, black thong. I unbuckled his pants and let his pants drop to his ankles.

He wore no underwear and his dick was erect. Thick, massive and veiny - *at least a two-fister.*

He stepped out of his shoes and pants at the same time and reached for me. This sexy motherfucker turned me around so quick it made my head spin.

"Touch your ankles." He softly spoke. His voice was deep and sensual as he caressed my ass.

I leaned down in front of the bed and grabbed my ankles. I looked through my legs in anticipation of his entry. He stroked his meat right behind my ass. My pussy quivered wanting to feel him.

I shook my ass back and forth to entice him.

"Mmmmm..." He said as he smacked my ass. Then this motherfucker took me to another level.

He kneeled down, pulled my thong to one side and buried his fucking face in my pussy with his tongue deep inside me. I instantly creamed.

"Aaaaaa.......mmmmmmm..." I leaned forward against the side of the bed and closed my eyes enjoying his tongue flexing deep inside my sweet spot. I wasn't moving as he fucked me with his tongue, sucking my juices licking my pussy like he was eating an ice cream cone. My legs shook as I reached up and held my ass cheeks open so he could have easy access.

"Mmmmmmmm." He hummed, making my nipples go instantly hard.

"Uuuuuu...mmmm...shit!" I moaned. And just as quick as he started, he stopped. He stood up and slid his dick deep inside my vajayjay. My back arched as he slowly entered me.

He stepped back, pulling me back with him. I raised up to the bed, grabbed the sides of the bed and assumed the position. He grabbed a hold of my waist with one hand and reached around grabbing my neck with the other.

Oooooo, he is a freaky motherfucker too!

He rammed his thick dick deep inside me with strong, long, slow strokes. Each stroke filled me completely. My mouth hung open, as he fucked me nice and easy.

Pure pleasure danced along my silky walls as he entered me. My pussy tightened as he filled me completely. He felt so damn good, I wanted to fucking cry. A euphoric ecstasy rolled across my body.

His shit was magical. He was a motherfucking unicorn!

"Uuhhh....Uhhh....uhhh...." I moaned softly as he fucked me. I could hear my juices sloshing as he pulled out and went back in.

"HHhhhmmmm," he groaned as he picked up the pace. His dick started getting hard - I swore that motherfucker grew too.

He grabbed my wrists and held them behind my back. I leaned forward and let him control me while he thrusted forcefully in and out, pulling me back to him after each exit. My ass popped against his pelvis and my pussy began to queef.

He was banging me hard and I was loving each bang. He touched my g-spot deep inside me so much, it hurt my stomach.

This motherfucker was beating my shit up! I loved it!

As I closed my eyes and fully submitted and allowed myself to just let go. My gates opened and I flowed everywhere.

"Aaaaaaaa..aaaaaaaa.aaaaaaa..aaaaaaaaaa!" I climaxed and squirted against the bed. Hearing me cum, he shot his load.

"UUuuuuu.....Uuuuuuu....UUUUHhhhhhhh!" I could feel him bust a nut deep inside. He continued to ram me until he released every drop. He slapped my ass as he slowly removed himself from me.

"Babygirl," he said softly. I turned around and sat on the bed. He pulled off a black condom, tied it in a knot and threw it in the trash can nearest the bed. "You somethin' else," he smiled.

"So are you. Is this how you meet your females all the time?" I said sarcastically.

"You got jokes too, funny. Unfortunately no. I don't meet *anyone* like this," he said, fastening his pants and grabbing his shirt off the floor.

"I understand," I said, picking up my dress. "But you make sure to carry condoms, that's good." I said.

He looked at me. Yeah, I peeped that. It's all good though, I was very appreciative.

"Well, you never know. As you can see," he said, walking over helping me tie my dress.

"This is true. Well played." I said looking at him. He was still sexy as fuck.

"You're beautiful," he said, staring at me.

"Thank you. You already know you look good, I ain't gotta tell you. I'm sure you've heard that already tonight." I smiled as I sat back on the bed.

He smiled and nodded in agreement. I was right again. "You are correct. But it's nice to hear it coming from a beautiful female like you," he smiled. I blushed. He knew exactly what to say.

This brotha was smooth.

"Do you want to leave first or should I?" He said motioning towards the door.

"You go ahead, I'm gonna use the bathroom real quick." He stopped before going out the door.

He looked at me and smiled. I returned a small smile.

"Nice meeting you," he said, opening the door, walking out and closing it behind him.

And that was it.

It was over just as quickly as it started.

And just as secretive. The way I wanted it.

Mr. No Name. He was good.

I could go home now. Nothing else was here for me tonight.

It was early as fuck in the morning when someone decided it was a good idea to bang on my fucking door. I jumped out the bed, trying to figure out whose bitch ass I was about to beat. I grabbed the baseball bat from the side of the door and swung it open, ready to swing on a bitch.

It was Monica. *Crying.*

"What the fuck, Bitch, what happened? What's wrong?" I said putting down the baseball bat and opening the door wider. She came in bawling, crying her eyes out; snot bubbles - the whole nine.

"It's Franklin bitch! He cheated!" She *screamed-cried* as she sat down on my couch. That didn't sound right.

Did she say Franklin cheated?

"Wait, what?" I asked again sitting next to her. "Run that by me again?"

"Franklin cheated with some bitch in the house!" She said, getting irritated.

"You caught them?"

"No,"

"I don't think he would do it at his own party, girl? Besides, you were there. Why would he risk doing some shit like that?"

"He got all these bitches trying pay *him* to fuck them! They be throwin' pussy left and right," she said trying to gain her composure.

"But you know Franklin is dedicated to yo' ass, why you trippin'?"

"He's a man, Siedah! C'mon now, you already know!" She yelled sarcastically.

"Yeah but, c'mon Monica. Has he ever given you any indication that he was dipping out on you?" I asked knowing good and well he did not.

When I say Franklin is devoted to her, I mean that shit. This motherfucker knows what he got. He makes sure ain't nobody gonna tap that shit. He takes care of Monica very well.

"Hmmphf," she refused to listen.

"You can't come up with a time, can you bitch?" I said, smiling at her.

"So what? He fucked someone in our room!" She said, closing her eyes.

"Bitch, you stupid." I said looking at her like she was fucking crazy.

"I'm for real, Siedah!"

"Monica, all dem bitches know betta to fuck with Franklin. They know how crazy yo' ass gets. Them bitches ain't stupid enough to do some shit like that at your fucking place,"

"Well a bitch did! He fucked her Monica in our bedroom!" I looked at Monica and tilted my head. It was then when I realized, I used a bedroom to fuck Mr. No Name. I didn't know it was *that* room.

"How you know?"

"I found a condom, bitch. WE DON'T USE CONDOMS!" She screamed getting upset all over again.

I started laughing. Monica looked at me like I was fucking crazy.

"Bitch, what you laughing at! I'm fucking serious!"

"Did you tell Franklin?" I asked, hoping she hadn't said shit to him yet.

"Naw, I ain't told him yet. He had to fly out this morning. I can't get a hold of him."

"Where did you find it?" I asked.

"This motherfucker threw it in the trash can next to the fucking bed! He fucked dat bitch in my bed!" She yelled.

I giggled again. "Don't say shit to him."

"Why? What you thinking?" Monica perked up as if she was waiting for me to reveal a revenge move.

"It wasn't him." I said. Monica looked at me totally bewildered.

"How the fuck you know?"

"Was it a black condom?" I asked.

"Yeah...how the fuck..." Monica sat up.

"I used your room. I ain't know it was your bedroom though. I just got snatched in." I said smiling, letting her in on my secret.

"Snatched in? What the fuck?" She said and then I saw it click all over her face. *Bitch, are you serious? Wit' who?*

"I don't know," I replied. Monica scrunched her face up like I was lying. "Seriously...I don't know."

"How you gonna fuck a nigga and don't know him?" She asked.

"I didn't get his name."

"Why not?"

"It was just an unexpected, spontaneous and random Fuck." I said, honestly.

"Bitch, I can't stand you! You had me thinking Franklin cheated on me!" She said, wiping the tears from her eyes.

I laughed so hard tears fell from my eyes. She leaned over and slapped my arm.

"I'm sorry, I should have told you. I watched him throw it in the trash. My bad." I said.

"Bitch, you make me sick," she said, rolling her eyes. "Well, was it good at least?"

"Yes it was. Oh my gawd!" I leaned back and slapped my leg.

"Bitch, do tell!" she said, opening her bag and pulling out a bottle of champagne. "You got some orange juice?"

This bitch always comes prepared.

. . . .

MARCUS

. . . .

AFTER THE PARTY, I went back to doing what I do, which is making music, beats, sounds - creating a musical language. It was nice to be out meeting people in the industry, rubbing arms with niggas I've admired in the business since I started. I loved to see my black brothas and sistahs doing the damn thang - *together*. And not out here doing some stupid shit, we got enough negative stereotypes that can last a lifetime.

It's time to create some new stereotypes - if this shit needs to be categorized. All I know is my mother did her best to raise a black boy in the City of Chicago; trying not to lose me to the streets. She didn't, I was a good kid. I had my moments though, but on the up and up, I stayed out of trouble. Otherwise my mother would beat the black off my ass - she did not play.

. . . .

YET IT FELT GOOD TO be out with people at the party that had a lot going for them and they were all there getting to know other people, trying to connect and help each other grow. We were *ALL* in this shit together so we might as well help each other out!

I didn't get her name.

She's been on my mind since I left. There were so many motherfuckers in that damn place, I don't even know if Franklin or Monica knew her.

She was fine as hell. Her dreads were cute and she was a redbone, slightly on the yellow side. She looked like she might have some Creole in her blood; her lips were so full. She felt so good. She was a freak.

She blew my motherfucking mind.

I picked up the phone and called Franklin, he had to know who she was.

"What up boy, what it do?" Franklin answered. I could hear him in the studio working.

"Ah man, I ain't wanna stop you."

"Nah, nah man, we good. We're taking a break, what up?"

"Dawg," I started and stopped. I instantly thought of her in that room. The vision of us fucking replayed in my head.

"Hello?" he asked.

"Yeah, man. My bad, hey got a question dawg."

"What up nigga shit," he said getting impatient.

"There was a girl at the party," I started. Franklin interrupted.

"Ahhh shit, here you go again."

"Nah man, listen. There was this girl, fine as hell at the party,"

"A'ight, what's her name?"

"I don't know," I answered. It got quiet on the phone. I could hear Franklin get up and leave out the room.

"Fuck you mean, you don't know?" he replied.

"I didn't get her name dawg, okay?"

"A'ight well what does she look like?" he asked.

"She was about 5'7" or 5'9", light skinned but almost redbone, you know. Oh and dreads, she got dreads,"

"Nigga," he started. I could hear him taking a puff over the phone. "That's half the females up in there," he finished.

"I know," I said feeling defeated. I don't know why I couldn't stop thinking about her.

"Well what about her?"

"I fucked her." I said openly.

"What?"

"I fucked her." I repeated.

"When?"

"The night of the party." I answered.

"Damn, where?" Franklin asked, sounding curious.

"In one of y'all rooms, nigga."

"Oh Wow, for real? Damn Dawg!" Franklin said, getting excited. "And you didn't get her name?"

"No dude! That's what I'm saying!" I said, accepting that I may not find her again.

"Wooooow dawg, I'm sorry man," he said, feeling my pain. "Well, it's not like she was the one, dawg. There will be others,"

"I don't know, brah. It's just something else about her, though. "

"What you mean?"

"She seem the type of girl that wouldn't mind gettin' down every once in a while,"

"Like a fuck bunny?"

"Yeah, but she was different, like fancy but still hood." I said trying to describe her.

"I don't know who the fuck you talkin' 'bout right now," he said laughing.

"Fuck it. Well hopefully she'll show up at the my album release party,"

"Yeah, I'm sure *they* will," he said.

"They?" I asked.

"Yeah, you know she is gonna come."

"That's what I just said," I said, trying to figure out if Franklin was talking to me.

"I wasn't talking about your mystery lady, dude." he said. "I said you know *she's* gonna come to the release party."

I knew what he meant then. I had forgotten about her.

"Shit," I said, getting upset. "It's all your fucking fault for that one." I said.

"Dude, how was I supposed to know she would do some crazy shit." Franklin pleaded his case.

"I know."

"But she did sing on one of the singles." Franklin stated.

"Fuck it. I don't care," I said, trying to ignore him. "Dude, Monica ain't said none of her girls was looking for someone?"

"Nope, she ain't said shit to me," I heard someone call Franklin's name in the background. "A'ight man, I gotta bounce, I'll holla at you later,"

"A'ight dude, peace."

Franklin just blew the fuck out of me. I had forgotten all about my ex, Justine. She was my high school sweetheart. We were supposed to get married.

I proposed to her. She broke my heart

She cheated. And got pregnant.

I thought it was mine. I was excited to have a little person - half of me and half of her.

I was *NOT* the father.

••••

I WAS HEADING HOME from the studio when my phone rang. Her ears must have been ringing all day because the bitch had the audacity to call me.

"Hello," I said, with no feeling whatsoever.

"Hello Marcus," she said, waiting for me to say something else.

"Hello Justine." The silence on the phone was deafening.

"I heard the release party is this weekend," she said, trying to hold a conversation.

"You heard, huh?"

"Marcus, it doesn't have to be this way."

"You right, you don't have to call me for shit you already know."

"Well nigga, you didn't have to answer the phone." she snapped. She was right, I didn't. Yet, I did.

"Why are you calling me anyway?"

"I was just trying to figure out what time the party starts so I can pop by," she said.

"Call Franklin!" I suggested.

"I did, his ass didn't answer the phone. That's why I called you."

"I don't know.," She knew the fucking time. She just liked playing fucking mind games.

"You don't know when the party starts, Marcus? You and Franklin are inseparable, Nigga please."

"I'm not doing this with you, Justine." I was getting irritated.

"You must got some bitch wit' you." Justine blurted. And here she goes. It's always, *I got some bitch* laying up on me.

"Why you always worried about who I'm with?" I asked because she would always say that type of shit.

"Who is she, Marcus?"

"Bitch, I wouldn't tell you if I did!" I said, hanging up. I was done with this conversation.

Justine called me back and I just ignored her. I need to block her.

• • • •

ABOUT AN HOUR LATER, Franklin called me back asking about Justine.

"Dude, Justine coming ain't she?" Franklin quipped.

"Why you say that?"

"Cuz she called me like fifty times asking me what bitch you laid up with," he said, chuckling over the phone.

"This shit ain't even funny dawg, this bitch is crazy." I said, shaking my head and closing my eyes.

"You got with her."

"Yeah but she wasn't like this."

"Not until after you broke up with her." Franklin replied.

"Did I have a choice?" I asked.

"Naw, not really. She fucked up, so that's on her. But this shit is new," he said.

"Nigga, that was a year ago! What the fuck!" I yelled.

"I know dawg, I don't know what to tell you, bruh. If your mystery lady comes by, you betta lock the door." He laughed.

"You stupid as fuck man." I laughed.

Siedah

It had been a nice little minute for Franklin's next party to come around. Of course Monica was begging me to come through. She didn't have to beg too hard this time, I was actually looking forward to going.

I was hoping to run back into Mr. No Name again. I had planned my outfit carefully for an impromptu meeting. I wore a red, one shoulder, cut out body con dress that accentuated all of my curves matched with a pair of black strappy heels. I was planning to leave an impression, just like he left on me.

• • • •

I COULDN'T GET THIS nigga out my mind. I caught myself at work, lost in thought thinking about him and what we did in Monica's bedroom. That shit was *so* good. I hadn't had it like that in a long time. And I wanted it again. And again. And again.

As I stepped through the door, I was on a mission to find Mr. No Name and find out who he was. Like always, it was wall to wall people - *everywhere*. It was a slightly different crowd this time. Not so many business people were there or they had left by the time I arrived.

Smoke hovered in the air as I saw clouds floating between the rooms as I walked to the kitchen to get something to drink. On my way back, I noticed a few of the same people hanging out in the same places they were last time. As I take a sip of my Corona, Monica finds me in the crowd, leaning by the wall.

"Siedah!" She screamed my name across a crowded room. No one flinches. I waved to her and she motions me to come her way. I laughed and shook my head. She looked pissed as she put her hands on her hips. I laughed while she was looking for a way to get over to me as I moved closer to her yet out of her sight.

Monica was a great hostess, she loved to help Franklin with his parties. She had a knack of making sure everyone was happy, every cup was filled and every blunt was smoked. I had finally made it back behind Monica and found a spot off to the side where she wasn't paying attention to me but everyone else. She was happy as she sat on Franklin's lap, his arm wrapped around her waist. They made a good couple together, I thought as I watched them from a distance. As I stood in the shadows drinking my beer, a shadowy figure came and stood next to me.

"Hey sexy," a deep, sultry voice whispered in my ear. I turned to come face to face with Mr. No Name.

"Hey," I said, smiling back. "Are you watching me again?"

"Yep, since you came in," he smiled, moving closer so I could hear him over the music that was blaring throughout the house.

"So you like watching people, huh?" I asked while taking a sip of beer.

"Only the interesting ones," he replied, taking a sip of his Heineken.

"Oh I see," I blushed. "How was *I* interesting?"

He smiled and stared at me for a minute before he answered, "You were hilarious,"

"Me? How?"

"You did the exact same thing when you arrived tonight. You try to hide and fade into the background, like me and people watch," he answered. He was right.

"You saw me hiding?"

"Yeah, I did. I saw you hiding from Monica and me,"

"Well that was before," I said.

"Before what?"

"Before I met you." I said. He chuckled and leaned in closer to my ear.

"We never met, we just fucked," he said whispering in my ear so close, his lips grazed it. It made my vajayjay quiver. She wanted more.

"Yeah we did," I said looking back at him.

"You look good Mama. This dress fits you just right."

"Thank you, you look good yourself wearing RL all over huh?" I said, as he wore a pair of RL camo canvas cargo pants, a pair of suede boots and a RL hoodie over a nice navy blue button up.

"Yeah, I am," he chuckled. "Well, it's nice to meet you. My name is Marcus," he said, holding out his hand for me to shake.

I slowly took his hand and held it in mine. "Nice to meet you Marcus, I'm Siedah."

"Siedah?" he asked.

"Yes."

"That's a beautiful name," he said, staring directly at me. He held and kissed the back of my hand, never leaving eye contact.

My thoughts go back to the moment in the bedroom the last time we saw each other.

The sexual tension was starting to build again as I stood close to him, feeling his breath glide across my shoulder.

As I drank the rest of my beer, I wondered if he was thinking about it too.

He finished his beer just after me. He took my bottle along with his and walked to the trash can nearest the wall. I watched him as he walked back to where I was. His swagger was delicious.

He had his gaze fixed directly on me. His eyes locked with mine.

I couldn't look away. I could feel the heat building between my thighs.

He licked his lips slowly as he approached me.

"What you thinking?" he asked.

"You already know," I answered. He blushed and looked away.

He leaned in closer to me. "Meet me in 10 minutes at our spot," he said as he walked away, joining Franklin and a few other guys who were drinking and smoking.

• • • •

I SLOWLY STARTED WALKING towards the room, trying not to bring attention to myself. Monica was entertaining other people so I was good for a few minutes before she would start looking for me again. As I walked to the hallway leading to the bedroom, I weaved myself in and out of people who were just standing around having a good time. I caught the eye of some chick leaning against the wall in the hallway, holding an entire bottle of wine and a glass. I guess she wanted her own shit to drink. I slipped into the door across from her and waited for Marcus to enter.

I turned on a small lamp in the corner so I could at least see him a little bit better this time around. I heard the door knob turn and the door opened slowly. I waited off to the side of the armoire waiting to see if Marcus was the one entering the room. I saw his camo pant leg enter the room and I knew it was him.

He stepped in and closed the door. I watched him as he waited for his eyes to adjust to the darkness.

"Siedah," he whispered and I stepped out from behind the armoire and walked over to him.

"Hey Marcus," I said.

He cupped my face in his hand and planted a kiss upon my lips. His lips were so juicy as I sucked and bit his bottom lip. He tongue danced with mine as he kissed me deeply while I grabbed the sides of his hoodie.

He walked with me backwards to the bed behind me. I scooted on the bed, he removed his shoes and followed. He pushed my short dress up to my waist, revealing my g-string. He grabbed the sides and pulled them off my legs, putting them in his pocket.

He unbuckled his pants and pulled them, sans boxers *again*, down to his knees. He grabbed my legs and pulled me forward as he leaned down and buried his face in my pussy.

"Uhhh … .Uhhh…..ooooo…," I moaned as he licked around my fleshy folds, sucking my nectar as it was flowing well before he entered the room.

"You're so wet," he said as he raised his head.

"I was hoping I would see you," I said looking at him and touching my twins, which were easily freed from my dress.

"And you did," he said as he crawled up between my legs and spread them wide, with my heels still strapped on my feet.

Marcus leaned down and grabbed a hold of me around my waist and flipped me around, landing on top of him while he laid on his back. This motherfucker was smooth.

I liked Marcus. We were compatible. He made me interested.

He placed a black condom on his dick while I waited. I straddled him and eased down onto his thick dick; I felt his head slowly spread my lips as he crossed my threshold.

"Hmmmm....Hmmmm... Hmmmm," he moaned as I eased down to the base and rested my ass on his pelvis and thighs.

He grabbed my ass as I started gyrating and moving my hips in circles, making sure my pussy took him all the way in when I pressed my ass down against him. I threw my head back as he sat up and grabbed my twins.

He pushed them together and sucked my nipples at the same time, Making my river flow freely over his dick. He sucked and bit them individually, sending chills all over my body.

"Aaahhh....aaaaahhh...aaaahh," I moaned as I rocked back and forth. Marcus started grunting the more I moved as I felt his dick throb inside me.

"Mmm....mmmm....mmmm....babygirl....shit...," he moaned as he rocked me back and forth on his dick. "Ride this dick baby girl....ride it,"

I planted my feet flat on the bed and bounced up and down on his dick. He leaned back to watch himself disappear and reappear. My ass started clapping against him as I basically started twerking on his dick. His shit was so good. I felt his dick get harder and I was close to climax.

He sat up and grabbed my ass as I bounced faster on his meaty shaft. I leaned down and kissed him hard as I began to release my cream.

"Aaaaaaaaahh......aaaaaaaahhhhhhhh......aaaaaaaaaaaaaaaaaaaa!" I moaned as I let it all go. I wasn't sure if anyone heard outside the room or not but I let it out.

"Yeah babygirl, cum for me.....uuuuhhhh.....cum all over......uuhhhhh.....uuuuhhh...," Marcus moaned. He was ready to bust his nut as I was still going.

He grabbed my ass and bounced me harder as he climaxed.

"Ahhhhhhhhhhh.....aaaaaaaaaaaaaaaahhhhhhhhhhh!" he moaned loudly. We held each other close as we rode the pleasure train together; I could feel his dick pulsating deep inside me.

Just as the climax subsided, the inevitable happened.

The door flew open.

We both looked to see who had come in. I focused and realized it was the chick that was in the hallway - *With the wine bottle.*

"Who the fuck is this bitch, Marcus!" she yelled.

• • • •

SIEDAH

• • • •

I WAS IN AN UNCOMPROMISING position when this bitch decided to bust into the room. She looked pissed off standing in the middle of the room *still* with the wine bottle.

She was drunk. And mad.

"Who the fuck are you? His girlfriend?" I said, still straddling Marcus. We had just finished and this bitch wanted to take it from zero to 100 real quick.

She looked at me like I had asked her a question that she didn't know the answer to.

"What's it to you?" she replied putting her hands on her hips.

Yet again, another bitch that don't know how to let go from a nigga.

"I take that as a *No*," I said as I released myself from Marcus and crawled to get off the bed while keeping my eye on her.

Then suddenly Franklin and Monica came busting through the door as Marcus got off the bed while fastening his pants.

"Oh Shit!" Franklin said as he entered quickly and stopped.

"Fuck Franklin, I told you to keep an eye on her man!" Marcus yelled pointing at the chick.

"My bad, dawg," he chuckled, turning towards Monica who was just wrapping her head around the entire incident. "She got away from me."

"Wait," Monica said, walking over to me while I adjusted my dress. " Bitch, is he the one you were telling me about?" she asked.

"Shhh!" I shushed her as Marcus smiled at me.

"Who the fuck are you?" The chick asked again.

"Bitch please, don't worry about it!" Marcus yelled.

"Justine, you need to just chill girl." Monica turned towards her. "You and Marcus ain't even together anymore, so why the fuck are you tripping?" Everybody looked at her and she glared at me.

"Bitch." she spoke.

"I got your bitch - *Bitch*," I said, looking dead at her ass. She rolled her eyes and looked at Marcus.

"Can I talk to you Marcus?" she asked.

"No." he said.

"Justine, why don't we take you outta here and get you a bit sober 'cuz you're making yourself look real stupid right now." Monica said as she walked over to Justine and guided her out the room.

Franklin looked at me and smiled.

"Siedah," he said, bowing his head a bit.

"Franklin," I smiled. He looked at Marcus and tilted his head.

"This her?" He asked Marcus, pointing at me.

Marcus looked at me standing there looking back at him, "Yup, this is her." Franklin smiled and shook his head in approval while he moved to the door.

"Well I'll let y'all do - y'all," he pointed at us as he backed out the door.

And then there was us - *again*.

We stood in the dimly lit room, adjusting ourselves for a conversation.

"We gotta stop meeting like this," he finally said. Marcus shook his head and chuckled.

"I was just thinking the same thing," I said, adjusting myself, making sure my titties were in my dress correctly. "So, who is the chick?"

"Oh, yeah, sorry 'bout that," he said as he walked over and stood in front of me. His gaze melted into my soul. "That's my ex, Justine. She's a lil...,"

"A little hurt?" I interrupted. He looked at me and smiled. He expressed so much confidence it was scary.

"By her own means," he started. He looked away and started again. "She cheated on me and got pregnant."

"Ouch, I'm sorry." I felt his pain. He still carried it. "Y'all must have been together for a minute,"

"Over 10 years," he said, standing up and raising his head. "But enough about her. That's over. I need to know about you," he stepped closer.

I loved his confidence. He had what I needed and he seemed cool with the meet ups. I like a man who knows what he wants.

"Ok, so what you talking?" I said, revealing my curiosity.

I didn't need titles. I didn't need to meet people other than the ones we know in common.

I didn't need feelings. I just needed sex.

"Tell me what you want," he said, kissing my neck. I felt his tongue lick around my ear and feel a slight bite on my ear lobe.

A chill raced across my shoulders and the back of my head making goosebumps form on my upper arms. My nipples awakened and hardened; his desire resonated through my body in a way that his voice made love to my ears.

"You," I said as I leaned forward and kissed the tattoo on his neck. Marcus inhaled deeply against my neck. "On the regular," I finished.

"How regular?" He said, planting a small kiss on my lips as he slid his hands around my waist, pulling me closer. His hands moved down to my ass and squeezed both cheeks at the same time.

I slipped my tongue inside his mouth deep and quick and then I pulled back. " 3 times a week." I said looking at him.

He stepped back and stared at me. He crossed his arms in front of him. He was trying to see if I was serious.

"For real?" he asked.

"Yeah."

"3 times a week?"

"Yeah," I answered. "No feelings, No commitments. Just sex."

"And you good with that?" Marcus asked, raising his eyebrows.

"Yeah." I answered. He shook his head and thought about it. He looked at me, chuckled and nodded in approval.

"One more thing," he added.

"What's that?"

"You're mine. No one else's. You fuck me only," he requested.

"Same goes for you." I rebutted. He shook his head and smiled.

"Deal." He said, stepping forward and planting a soft kiss on my lips.

"Deal." I answered, kissing him back.

• • • •

WHEN WE STEPPED OUT the door, the party was still going on as if nothing happened. The incident was only known by those who were involved, leaving everyone else clueless. Monica found me outside smoking on a blunt because I needed to clear the air in order to wrap my brain around what just happened.

"Bitch," she said, walking onto the back patio. "So Marcus is the one that you fucked, *yet again* in my bedroom," she said taking the blunt from between my fingers.

"Yes. Sorry, my bad." I winced and shook my head.

"Don't be, he's the one I wanted you to meet," she said casually. I looked at her as she inhaled deeply on the blunt.

"Are you serious?"

"Yup, Ironic how y'all just happen to meet each other. You know what that is right?" She smiled while passing the blunt to me.

"Coincidence?" I said trying not to go *there* with Monica, because she believes all in that *'Destiny'* shit.

"Nope, it was *'Fate'.*" Monica said, blowing out the smoke.

"Ah, here we go."

"Bitch, you ain't gotta believe me. I know that shit when I see it."

"Yeah, yeah." I said, inhaling the essence while a trail of smoke circled above my head.

"Y'all connected without my help. Y'all were fated to meet."

"Whatever." I snickered. I smiled at the fact that she had picked him out to meet me.

Was it really fate? I don't think fate would have all this drama added in the mix.

"So what is up with that chick, Janet?" I asked. Monica choked on the blunt.

"Justine," she said laughing.

"Oh my bad. Yeah her, what's the deal with them?"

"She was his girlfriend for a minute. They had been high school sweethearts. Everywhere Marcus went, Justine was there. Marcus was just getting growing in the industry and she laid a track on a song for Franklin. The girl can blow, though. She got pipes." She pulled on the blunt again before passing it back to me.

"He said she cheated."

"Girl, yes!" She said, blowing out the smoke and turning towards me. "Marcus had to go somewhere out of town when I think it happened. We had a party and she was trying to get herself noticed and shit, and you already know how some of these females are," she said scrunching up her face.

"Yeah, they will pass the pussy out if they think the guy could get them in on a track or to rub elbows with someone." I said looking at some of the females walking around the party.

They were like cattle. Just moving slowly from place to place to get attention. It works sometimes though, but I wouldn't want to be known for that.

"Girl yeah, so Marcus was gone and so she dipped out with someone who made some false promises. Tapped 'dat ass that night." She raised her eyebrows.

"How'd you find out?" I asked with my eyes bulging.

"'Cuz dude called Franklin and told him. He said that chick, Justine was all over him when he told her that he would get a song for her to sing," she said.

"Damn."

"Yup and she fucked him - *raw*. That's just nasty,"

"Yeah, but maybe they didn't have any condoms. You know, spontaneous?"

"Bitch, e'erbody got sandwich bags!" Monica said with a straight face. I laughed so hard, I couldn't hold the smoke.

"You stupid as fuck." I smiled, shaking my head.

"So she got preggers from dude and tried to say it was Marcus's kid. He was happy, he thought he was about to have a little Marcus running around here."

"Wow, how'd he find out?" I asked.

"Franklin told Marcus to get a DNA test done because he had heard some things about her while he was gone and there may be a possibility the kid wasn't his," she said, passing back the last of the blunt.

"Did he believe him?"

"At first he didn't, but then he said he noticed her acting differently. And he was hearing things from other people, but of course she would deny it and said they were jealous 'cuz Marcus got with her and the others couldn't."

"Wow, so she was fucking around on him?"

"Probably, people get desperate to break into the business,"

"Damn," I said, putting out the remainder of the blunt. "So where she at now?"

"Last I checked Marcus was talking to her, trying to get her to either chill or leave 'cuz she will kill a vibe,"

"As long as the bitch don't come my way, I'm cool." I said as I glided back to the patio door with Monica following behind me,

"I know that's right."

· · · ·

JUST AS MONICA AND I stepped back into the house, Marcus approached us.

"Where's Justine?" Monica asked.

"She's around her somewhere, probably watching me at the moment," he said looking at me. I just stared at him. He looked like he was tired of dealing with her.

"So you got a stalker, huh?" I said playfully. He smiled and Monica shook her head.

"Well that's my cue. I'm gonna go find my man." She said as she trailed off looking for Franklin.

"Do you mind?" Marcus said, stepping close enough to me to smell his cologne again.

"Well to be honest," I started. "I do mind."

"Understandable," he said. "You wanna bounce?" he asked.

"What about the party?"

"I didn't come for the party," he said whispering in my ear as my eyes glanced around the room, landing on Justine, leaning against the wall sipping a drink while watching us from the dining room.

I smiled to piss her off, which worked as she tried to make her way towards us.

"A'ight, if you cool. Let's bounce." I said, looking at him. He smiled and leaned in for a quick kiss.

Marcus grabbed my hand and pulled me through the crowd. I watched Justine weave herself through the people on the other side of the house as we were saying goodbye to Monica and Franklin. He held my hand as we made our way to the door just as Justine reached it.

She stared at me as if to intimidate me. I smiled, chuckled a bit and shook my head. She dared not say anything to me as she faced reality. Marcus looked at her and kissed the back of my hand while staring directly at her. I could see the anger build inside her as she stared at us. Marcus opened the door and allowed me to go before him as he kept constant eye contact with her.

I'm sure she was fully aware of what I was getting from Marcus. Even if it wasn't a relationship, she knew how the sex was and I was getting *all* of it.

Chapter 5 - Reasons

MARCUS

I COULD TELL SIEDAH was a different type of female. She didn't flinch when it came to Justine. As a matter of fact, she was ready to throw hands if Justine got out of place. I really don't know why Justine is still trying to holla at me, I'm done with her on so many levels and she knows it.

I drove Siedah over to my loft to get away from the madness and to spend a little time with her. We decided on an agreement and I wanted to know the full details before I got involved as I don't need anyone catching feelings; I don't think I could handle another *'Justine'* situation.

"So what's this place?" Siedah asked as I pulled up outside of what looked like an abandoned warehouse.

"It's my place. I have a loft here. I figured we needed another spot to meet up so, this will work."

I said as I turned off the car.

"You live here?"

"No, well sometimes. It's my studio. I use it to make my music, but it has a loft bedroom just in case I work late at night."

"Do you work late a lot?"

"From time to time, I do. I want to be where Franklin is, so in order for me to do that, I have to work hard, which means

I have to put in the time." I said, opening the door and getting out. I walked around to the passenger door and opened it for her.

Siedah slid out of the car looking all good and shit. She made me curious because she was a bad bitch. She was not like any type of female that I had dealt with. She carried herself with a higher standard and I could tell she wasn't going to deal with any bullshit.

"Interesting." She said softly as I closed the door. I held her hand and led her to my studio loft. I opened the door, turned on the lights and invited her in.

"Make yourself at home." I said pointing to the lounge chairs and couches in the sitting area. "Do you want something to drink?"

"You got a Heineken?"

"A woman after my own heart." I opened the fridge, pulled out two bottles of Heineken and took off the caps.

"So how long have you known Franklin?" Siedah asked as I passed her the beer. I sat down next to her as she took a sip.

"I've known him for a minute now, he got me started in music. How about you? How long have you known him?"

"For as long as he has been with Monica. She's my girl, we grew up together,"

"Oh ok, that's cool y'all still hang out."

"Yeah, she keeps me grounded so to speak. Well, sometimes she tries to hook me up." She looked at me and gave me a wink. I chuckled because Franklin was trying to do the same thing, yet I didn't know Siedah was the female he was trying to introduce me to.

"Yeah, I feel you." I said, looking at her and taking a swig of my beer.

"So interesting night huh?"

"Very. I'm sorry. I didn't expect Justine to...."

"No worries. I just gotta keep my guard up 'cuz I don't think she's done." she said, taking another swig.

She might be right. I didn't expect Justine to be like that especially since she was the one who dipped out on me. But just like a bitch to try and come back after she fucked up, begging to be forgiven.

· · · ·

"TRUE, I'M SORRY." I chuckled, shaking my damn head. I really didn't think she would go that route.

"That's all your fault," she said laughing. I looked at her like she was crazy. "You shouldn't have fucked her so good." .

I laughed out loud for real. "My bad, I just do what I do." She laughed. She smiled and drank her beer.

"So Siedah," I said as she got comfortable on the couch, taking her shoes off and stretching her legs out across towards me. "Tell me about you, why would you agree to a deal like ours? I'm curious."

She sat, smiled and tilted her head. She was mysterious and I was interested in finding out what her reasons were. She was a fine, black woman. She could be walking through a room, saying not one word, making no eye contact to anyone and at least 3 niggas dicks would move in their pants, wondering who she was.

I was one of those niggas.

"Well, I just don't like dealing with feelings. That shit is too much drama that I don't want. So I avoid it." She said, taking the last swig of her beer. "What about you?"

"Justine." That was all I needed to say. It was my honest truth. She was my one and only reason.

"Damn. I feel you though. See? Feelings." Siedah pointed at me as I finished my beer. She got up off the couch, grabbed her beer bottle and reached for mine. No questions asked. She just became as comfortable as I had asked as she threw the bottles away in the trash and grabbed two more out of the fridge.

"You got any alcohol?" She asked as she opened the beers.

I got up off the couch and walked to the kitchen. She watched me as I reached over her and opened the cabinet above the sink. Stocked and full of alcohol.

Grey Goose. Captain Morgan. Crown Royal. Jack Daniels. Patron. New Amsterdam. A plethora of alcohol.

"Well fuck me." She said looking at all of the bottles filling the two cabinets.

"I already did." I smiled.

"Yes sir you did," she smiled. "Can you pass me the Patron?"

"Of course." I grabbed two shot glasses from the top shelf along with the bottle.

"So she was your longest relationship huh?"

"Yeah," I poured us double shots filling it all the way up to the rim. "That shit was enough man."

"I can't even imagine. I've never stayed with anyone that long at all." She said, downing the shot and chasing it with a few sips of the Heineken.

• • • •

SIEDAH WOULD MAKE A nigga commit for real. *I just can't.* She could end up just like Justine and I couldn't have two bitches on me like that. That would ruin my dating game for the rest of my fucking life.

But, where has this woman been all my life? Why haven't I met her before meeting Justine?

• • • •

"YOU MUST HAVE BEEN hurt or something?"

"Nah, never stayed around long enough to get hurt," she said, pouring another shot. I downed mine and chased it with the beer. "I learned how to read the signs on when to get out." She smiled and down the shot.

Straight, no chaser.

"Damn girl, you know how to drink huh?"

"Yeah, I used to hang out with Monica and her brothers, they were always drinking. Worked up a tolerance." She quipped while drinking her beer.

"A'ight." I smiled. She looked cute, her butter pecan skin just smooth and glowing. She looked happy with her life and didn't want any interruptions.

"Do you have a bluetooth speaker? I wanna play some music." She asked while scrolling on her phone.

"Yeah," I walked over to the speaker sitting on the coffee table. "Try it now. It's called: Coffee Table." I said, telling her the name of the speaker.

"Damn you got a speaker in the shower and the bedroom huh?" She started looking at the locations of all the other speakers.

"I love music." I threw my hands up. I took a long swig on my beer as she smiled and shook her head.

She picked a nice song, *Fool Around*, by YAS and Taylor from Earth. Basically it describes us perfectly - *fooling around*. No commitments and No Feelings. Siedah was sexy as fuck as she closed her eyes and swayed her hips. She danced slowly holding her beer as she looked through her phone to pick another song. She softly sang as she scrolled - *the girl had pipes*.

"You sing?" I said walking over to her.

"For fun. Nothing serious,"

"You sound good though." I said. She smiled and took a sip of beer.

"Thanks." She picked another song. "You just wanna hear sounds coming out of my mouth."

I smiled. She was a smart chick with a smart ass mouth. I loved it. She made me smile. I felt I could be comfortable around her. She made me feel as if we had known each other for a long time.

"Yeah, pretty much." I smiled. She bumped me with her hip and I licked my lips. She had a nice ass peach, nice and plump.

"So Marcus, you gonna be okay with our arrangement?" she asked, looking at me.

"Yup. You?"

"Yup, as long as you don't fall in love." She was confident. I laughed as if she thought I was that easy. This was going to be a cake walk.

"Nah, that goes for you, 'cause I'm lovable." I said, rubbing all over myself. She laughed out loud which made me smile.

"Well, I'm irresistible, so don't fall for it."

"Ok Mama, I won't." I said walking over to her.

"Me either." She looked at me. I tipped her chin up and kissed her softly. She didn't resist me.

She melted right with me.

"Okay cool." Siedah walked away to retrieve her shoes. "It's getting late and I gotta work in the morning,"

"Why don't you stay here?"

"See, that's how it starts." She replied pointing at me.

"Ok, you're right. No staying over. Got it."

"Good."

"What about dinner? Can we do that sometimes?" I asked. I didn't want a date, but I don't want the woman to be hungry.

"Well I could always eat, I don't turn down free food. But it's not a date."

"Agreed," she grabbed the phone and walked over to me. "If you start to get feelings, you have to tell me."

"Me? Why me? You already know you are going to fall for me so stop playing."

"Please, In your dreams. I like your dick and your mouth, there is no love in between." she declared.

"Well damn, make me feel like a piece of meat." I said jokingly. I was cool with our agreement. I could see this lasting for a while.

We were straight forward, open and honest with each other. I hoped we could keep it that way. I grabbed my keys and walked her out to the car to drive her home.

The ride over to her house was a nice little ride, considering I lived near Chinatown and she lived near South Shore Cultural Center on the south side. Luckily, it was late at night and traffic was light. We rode in peace, music blaring through the speakers. We heard the likes of Kyle Dion, Ari Lennox and Giveon. James Vickery was singing my favorite - *Until Morning*, when I noticed her phone ringing in her lap.

She was looking out the window, watching the city go by at a steady pace and didn't notice it ringing. I glanced at her phone, it read: '*Psycho Asshole*'.

Interesting. Who the fuck was 'Psycho Asshole'? Did I want to know?

I was curious to the point I wondered if I needed to be concerned about my safety or hers for that matter. Was this someone who was a male version of Justine? Questions loaded my head the more the phone rang. She finally paid attention to her phone and ignored the call. As I was driving when I noticed her looking at me in my peripheral vision.

She wanted to make sure I didn't see who was calling.

Too late. I already saw it.

Siedah fascinated me. It made me want to dig deeper.

She was almost too perfect. But she had secrets and they were locked up tight.

It's okay, I'm not in a rush.

As we pulled up to the front of her building, she was softly singing Ella Mai, *Pieces*.

"Girl," I said as I put the car in park. "I'm gonna have to get you on a track." I said being impressed by her vocal skills.

"Whatever, " she smiled. She grabbed her phone, purse and keys. "Thank you for bringing me home. Make it home and text me when you get back."

"A'ight." I replied.

"I'll holla at you later." she said as she leaned over and gave me a quick peck on my lips. She opened the door and was gone.

I watched her ass sway back and forth as she walked to her condo building entrance. She was a piece of work and she made me want to know more. Siedah waved as she entered the door, I honked the horn and took off.

Next time, I'll find out about this, *Psycho Asshole*.

Chapter 6 - Messages

The next morning, I woke up tired as shit. I knew I wasn't going to be fully rested but I must admit, I had a good time last night. It was eventful to the point that I acted as if I didn't have a job that I work on a regular basis. I sat up and looked at the time; my watch vocally said it was early as fuck.

"Shit," I said out loud as I slowly walked to the bathroom to turn on the shower. I looked in the mirror; at least I was able to put my bonnet on correctly as I realized I had my sleep shirt on backwards and inside out. "I was way too tired to get this shit straight."

After my shower, I grabbed an *'Everything'* bagel and Vitamin Water:XXX from the kitchen. I had enough time to catch a ride with Monica if I could get a hold of her. She usually drives by my place on the way to work, so either I catch a ride with her or take the bus. If I'm running late, I'll hop in an uber or lyft.

"C'mon Monica, pick up the damn phone," I heard it ring three times. I grabbed my shoes and slipped them on while also trying to put on my earrings.

"Yes Bitch, I'm on the way," she finally answered.

"Where you at?" I asked so I could gauge how long before she would arrive.

"I'm just now passing Rainbow Beach." she replied.

"Oh ok, cool. I just gotta get my jacket and I'll meet you downstairs."

"A'ight, see you." Monica said and disconnected.

. . . .

SINCE I WAS NOT FEELING the heels today, I dressed more comfy given my hungover state. I didn't put my contacts in so I wore my glasses, a nice pair of wide legged jeans, a white sleeveless cropped sweater and a nice pair of Converse sneakers. I grabbed my trench coat, keys, messenger bag and slipped my phone in my back pocket as I hit the door.

Just as I hit the sidewalk, Monica was pulling up. I ran across the street and jumped in the passenger seat and we took off.

"Morning girl, thanks for the ride." I said, pulling my seat belt around me.

"Oooo don't you look comfy and classy," she said as she admired my outfit. "You must have had a long night." She blurted..

"Girl," I sang as I shook my head. "Wait, what happened at the party after we left?"

"Girl, Justine acted an ass and we had to put her drunk ass out."

"Are you serious?"

"Girl, I wish I could make this shit up," she shook her head. "This bitch is crazy, you betta watch your back."

"Bitch, you were the one who wanted me to hook up this dude."

"Yeah, 'cause Marcus is a really good guy, but I didn't know Justine had gone bat shit crazy."

"Uh, yeah." I said, raising my eyebrows.

"Yeah, but don't let that stop you, she ain't that crazy where she would physically do something to you, ya feel me?"

"Yeah well, she needs to think twice before doing anything stupid towards me." I responded. I didn't need or want to get into a physical fight with this female. But if it does get to that level, she would be in for an ass whooping like she has never had before in her life and I'll bet that on my mama.

"Yeah well, if she stupid enough to find out, then that's on her." Monica said as she drove around a few cars going a little slower than normal. "Let her fuck around and find out, you'll tap that ass for real."

I laughed and looked out the car window for a minute. Suddenly I got a text and it was from Marcus.

I smiled. Monica saw me. Shit!

"So who got you smiling over there?" She asked, nodding in my direction.

"No one." I said, trying to ignore her. Her nosey ass.

[Marcus] Good Morning Siedah, I hope you slept well. You said you don't mind a free meal so how about this place?

Marcus had included a picture of a Mexican Fusion restaurant that looked like a nice spot not far from Douglass Park, closer to the west side of Chicago.

[Siedah] That's cool. What time?

[Marcus] Seven

[Siedah] See you then.

． ． ． ．

"SO WHAT HAPPENED BETWEEN you and Marcus?" She asked. I knew she would.

"Nothing much, he took me over to his spot." I replied.

"Over to his studio?"

"Yeah."

"Oh ok, that's a nice little spot. I know he lives in a small apartment, but Franklin keeps telling him he just needs to stay at the studio."

"People do what they do." I muttered just as my phone started ringing.

Psycho Asshole displayed on my screen. Monica glanced and saw it as well.

"That motherfucker is *still* calling you? I don't know why you don't just block his ass."

"Girl," I said, rolling my eyes. "This motherfucker called me last night when Marcus was dropping me back off at my place."

"Dropping you off? You didn't stay that night?"

"No, that's not part of the deal." I answered as she pulled into a parking lot entrance and pulled a ticket.

"Oh shit, well fuck me!" Monica laughed and drove around to an available parking spot.

"Yeah, so I don't know why he's calling me." I really didn't. He was an ex who was upset because he didn't get a chance to break up with me - *first*.

Psycho Asshole was my ex by the name of Gerald Green. He is an egotistical, manipulative narcissist that believes he is God's gift to women. Don't get me wrong, the Brotha is fine, educated and knows his shit, but he has let a lot of women boost his big head ass up to the point he feels that women can't do any better than him even if they tried. Gerald feels a woman should never break up with him, he's too good for that. Therefore, he should be the only one to call it quits in his relationships.

"Girl, you already know why?" Monica turned off the car and grabbed her things. "You popped that pussy on him too good and then turned around and dropped his ass" She closed her door and looked at me. I grabbed my things out of the car and walked around to meet her.

"Yeah well, but he was getting really possessive."

"The magic of the pussy." She smiled, shaking her head..

"It's man's kryptonite!" I replied.

"I remember, he would get mad when you would come and hang with us at Franklin's house."

"I don't need anyone to tell my grown ass where I can and cannot go and who I can and cannot see." I said, bundling up the fall weather in Chicago as we walked out the exit to the parking lot.

"A'ight girl, well call me later. You need a ride later?" Monica asked as she started walking in the opposite direction.

"A'ight girl, I don't know, I'll let you know."

"Cool, bye girl. Have a good day at work!" Monica yelled and she was off walking to her job.

• • • •

I BURIED MYSELF IN my work; as an editor for a publishing company, I have the liberty of going over manuscripts of authors to 'proofread', fact checks and keeping the author stuck to a deadline. As I looked over and edited thousands of books, I never found one that fit my exact situation. I was interested in writing my story and how I get love but not be in love.

I was working on a manuscript when I received a text message from Psycho Asshole.

[Psycho] Hi Siedah

I saw the text message but did I want to humor myself to find out why was contacting me?

I was a glutton for punishment because my ass messaged him back.

[Siedah] Hi

[Psycho] You responded?

[Siedah] What do you want?

[Psycho] I need to talk to you.

[Siedah] Need? Why do you need?

[Psycho] Can I meet you for lunch?

[Siedah] No, I have plans.

[Psycho] With who?

[Siedah] Nope, we are not doing this.

[Psycho] Ok, my bad. But can we meet?

I ignored his text messages. I was not about to start something with him. Ignoring him was something that he didn't like. He started back calling me. I decided to go to the kitchen away from prying ears to take the call.

"Why are you bothering me?" I silently yelled into the phone.

"I miss you." he replied. I pulled the phone from my ear and looked at it as he could see the crazy look I was giving him.

"Um, what is wrong with you?"

"I messed up. Siedah, I've been missing you,"

"Gerald," I said, leaning back against the cabinets and closing my eyes. "We broke up 8 months ago. We haven't spoken since and now is when you realized that you missed me?" I said trying to make any sense of his shit, if it was at all possible.

"Yes, you've been on my mind for a while now." He said, trying to be sincere.

"Well, sorry. Not interested. Thanks for the offer." I said as I disconnected the call. He called back.

I ignored the call.

I don't know why I don't just block him. Again, I'm a glutton for punishment.

Fuck it, I know why. It's because I have fun messing with him. I love the mindfuck I give him.

He deserves it. He thinks he has some kind of possibility to get back with me because he still has a connection that could have been severed 8 months ago. But it wasn't a bad break up - it was just a break up. He went his way and I went mine. No words were said after I left his house. He didn't call me to see if I arrived home and I didn't call him to let him know I had arrived.

"Have you seen Siedah? I would love to fuck her so good." I heard someone in the hallway outside the kitchen. I didn't want to move and make a sound so I slowed my breathing and leaned in to listen.

"The black girl?" Another said surprisingly.

"Yes, she is beautiful. I would love to just feel her. You wouldn't?"

"I don't know. I've heard so many stories about black women and sex and their hair, it's..,"

"Every woman is different.," The interested guy interrupted inquisitively.

"Have you ever been with a black woman, Todd?" The second guy asked.

"No, but I would love to." He said as he turned the corner into the kitchen followed by his lackey, Paul.

I thought I would pass the fuck out at the look they gave me when they realized I had heard the entire conversation. They were surprised to see me standing there, listening. I've never seen white people turn - *whiter*. Todd looked as if he was about to faint and Paul just had the shocked deer in headlights look.

"Uhhhh..., um...uh." Todd stuttered as he tried to save face.

"Hey Todd." I sang looking at him, not breaking eye contact. I smiled and winked. I walked slowly out the kitchen giggling as I turned the corner. That should fuck with his head for a little bit, curious motherfucker.

C'mon over to the dark side. *Once you go black.....*

· · · ·

I COULDN'T WAIT TO get my ass out of work. As I was closing down my computer, I got a text message notification: it was Marcus.

[Marcus] Hey
[Siedah] Wassup
[Marcus] You hungry?
[Siedah] Yeah, you wanna snack?
[Marcus] I could always go for a snack. Are you leaving out?
[Siedah] Yup, about to walk out now.
[Marcus] I'll come and scoop you.
[Siedah] Cool.

· · · ·

MARCUS CAME AND PICKED me up shortly after he texted. As soon as I got in the car, I got a text from Gerald.

[Psycho] Who the fuck is that?

I looked at the phone and I couldn't believe what I had just read.

Was he watching me? I thought, looking around.

I ignored the text message and turned my attention to Marcus.

"Hey Beautiful." Marcus said as he locked the door.

"Hey you, how was work today?"

"It was good. I laid down a few tracks, I even got one for you."

"For me? To do what?"

"Sing."

"Whatever." I chuckled, rolling my eyes and folding my arms in front of me.

"We'll see whatever. I'll get you singing one way or another." He grinned..

"Another." I replied. He laughed and opened the middle console. It contained two pre-rolled blunts. "We got some time before dinner." He pulled one out and handed it to me.

"Cool," I said, taking the blunt and lighting the end. "So why do you want me to sing on a track? Are you trying to make Justine jealous by putting me on a track now and not her?" I asked playfully.

"Oh, you got jokes," he said with a small chuckle. "Naw, fuck Justine. You have a good voice Siedah and I want to lay it down with some beats I've been working on."

"Interesting, that's all you wanna lay down?" I said, feeling flirty. This would technically be our first meet up since we started our agreement.

"You should already know baby girl," he said pulling up to his studio. "I told you I could go for a snack and you have what I'm craving."

Marcus

I picked Siedah up from work and decided to have a little *'snack'* before we went to eat dinner. She looked cute, dressed down and casual. She looked like she could make anything look good. At the moment, I wanted her to make my bed sheets look good.

• • • •

I UNLOCKED THE DOOR, flicked on the lights and she walked into the space. I flipped a few switches and turned on a few lights around the loft to set the mood and atmosphere.

"Ok you got this shit set up in here huh?" She said, taking off her shoes and getting comfy.

"Yeah, you know how it is. I gotta make it nice." I said, walking over to her and kissing her lips. She melted in my hands. Her lips felt so good.

"Mmmm, I've been missing those lips." I kissed her again slowly, licking across her top lip.

"Mmm, I've got some other lips that's been missing your lips too."

"Oh yeah, well I gotta kiss them too." I pulled her closer as I kissed her deeply. I slid my hand around and grabbed her ass. She had just the right amount of ass that I could grab in one handful.

I stepped back as my dick started getting hard in my pants. "Let me turn on some music." I said as I walked over to my setup and tapped the screen to wake up my computer. I put a nice playlist that would give us at least 3 hours even though we only had 2.

I held her hand and guided her up the metal staircase to the loft area where I had a queen size bed available for such an occasion. This was going to be the first meet up, whereas we could enjoy each other in the moment and not worry about someone busting in to interrupt us.

Siedah stood before me as the lights flickered all around the perimeter of the place along with a colorful, rotating spotlight flashing against as we stood quietly in front of each other. I touched her shoulder and ran my finger down her arm. She stepped to me and kissed my neck sending a warm feeling down to my dick and awakening the monster within.

I removed my jacket and shirt and stood before her in my white tank top. She removed her white, cropped sweater revealing a red satin bra accentuating her voluptuous breasts. I leaned in and kissed her shoulder as she pulled me closer by my pants. She unbuckled my pants as I reached around and unfastened her bra letting her twins hang loose.

I stepped out of my pants and threw them to the side as she had stepped out of her jeans; she looked delicious as she stood there in her matching red satin panties.

"Damn girl," I said walking over to her, my dick was hard and standing at attention. "You look sexy as shit."

"Thank you," she said, taking a hold of my member. "You're not so bad yourself." She leaned in and licked my nipple.

Now, I never thought I would enjoy a female licking my nipples as I've had other chick try and it didn't do anything. But it was the way Siedah licked them, slow and sensual. She looked at me as she licked circles on my chest as she started stroking my shit in my underwear.

"Fuck, babygirl." I moaned as she had a nice grip and she felt good. She pulled down my underwear and I stepped out, kicking them to the side. I grabbed a condom out of my dresser and slid it on.

I kissed her hard and deep. She moaned as she sucked my tongue into her mouth and continued stroking me. She was making my shit hard as she pinched my nipple. She was some kind of freaky.

I wanted to feel her. I wanted to taste her. I wanted to fuck her, good. With no interruptions.

I quickly picked her up and dropped her down on the bed. She smiled and bounced in the middle of the bed. She made my bed sheets look damn good. Siedah sat up on the bed, resting herself on her elbows, looking at me - wanting me.

I reached and pulled the sides of her panties down and off her legs. She spread her long legs wide with her painted, pretty toes; I saw her pretty pussy asking me to come and give it a kiss. I crawled over to her between her legs and kissed her lips as he cupped my face. It was really nice kissing her. She would kiss me as if she couldn't get enough. She bit my bottom lip and looked at me wantonly.

She was ready.

I kissed her softly on her chest, licking between her breasts as I kissed down to her belly. She squirmed as I kissed the sides of her stomach.

"You ticklish?" I asked as I worked my way south on her stomach.

"Yeah, a bit." She said, holding the back of my head, my dreads locked between her fingers.

"That's cute." I smiled as I reached her mound. I leaned down and planted a kiss on the top and she moaned.

I was going to enjoy this.

I sucked my thumb and then rubbed her clit in slow circles and watched her legs fall to the side and her eyes close.

"Mmmm," she moaned softly. My dick hardened just hearing her moan.

I watched her as I continued in a circle with an occasional slip of the finger inside her spot quickly to gather some nectar to keep her clit slippery. She raised her ass as I circled faster and grabbed her twins - pinching her nipples.

I quickly repositioned myself and spread her fleshy folds and licked between them kissing her pearl. She shuddered at the touch of my tongue as it flicked across it quickly. I spread my tongue and licked again between her tulips from the top of her cave up to her doorbell.

"Mmmm....ahhh...ahhh mmm...,' she moaned and moved her ass while I continued to plant kisses between her legs.

She sat up and held my head between her legs as I lapped her profusely. I sucked her smooth lips as I licked up and down on her soft flesh.

"Mmmm...aahh...mmm Marcus," she whispered. She called my name. My dick stiffened. I wanted to feel her.

"Here I come, baby girl," I said, kissing up her inner thigh. I kissed her along her waist and she moved again, giggling as I kissed along the side.

"Marcus," she said giggling. "Still ticklish,"

"I know," I said, holding myself over her. "It's cute." I said. Her laugh was intoxicating. She reached around and grabbed my ass to pull me down towards her love cavern.

I aimed my member at her entrance and kissed her deeply as I plunged in deep in one full stroke.

'

"Uhhh," she said as she threw her head back. She held onto my waist as he watched my soldier dive deep inside her. "Shit baby." She looked at me while her two fingers played with her clit.

"That's right Mama, make it wet for me," I said as I stroked slowly and steadily making sure I hit the bottom.

"Uh..uh...uhh..uuuh..," she softly moaned as laid down on her sliding my dick in and out her wet sweetness.

"Mmph...mmph....mmppf..," I moaned. Siedah felt so good. It was like her silky walls vibrated against my shaft as I slid deep inside her. Each stroke created a wave of emotion that made me want to fuck her deeper.

She wrapped her arms around me, I felt her walls tighten around my shaft as her muscles massaged me from the inside. I looked down at her ass. I slowly stroked in and out, grinding upon entering her juiciness. She looked up at me our eyes connected as I fucked her with a steady stroke. I watched her and I saw how I was making her feel. She enjoyed feeling me inside her. She caressed my face.

She was unreal. She was unimaginable. Where had she been?

She looked in my eyes and kissed me deeply. She raised her hips off of the bed to meet me as we increased the pace.

"Marcus," she panted as I thrusted myself in her, hearing and feeling the sloppiness of her juices flowing over my dick. "Fuck me Marcus, uh...uhh.. Fuck me baby..," she begged.

"Mmmph....mmmpphff...mmphff..," I groaned as I wanted her to beg for more. I didn't want to give in just yet. "You want this dick baby?" I asked.

"Yessss...baby...ahhh..yess...," she moaned. I pulled out instantly and she shook. "Fuck!"

"You want this dick baby?" I asked I rammed it deep inside her, grinding as far as it could go.

"Yes!" She moaned loudly as she started grinding on my dick from underneath. She held onto her ankles and was spread wide.

I wrapped my arms underneath her hips pulled her to me as I rammed my dick deep inside hitting her spot each and every time. I slid in and out of her pussy as her juices were flowing all over my dick so much it glistened. Her twins bounced back and forth on her, with each banging connection.

"Uhhh...uhhh ... .uhhh ... .uhhh....," she moaned as we rocked back and forth like animals.

"Shit baby girl...aaahhhh...... .aaaahhhhh," my shit was getting hard as shit and I was ready to shoot my load.

I pumped faster as she moaned with ecstasy making me wild. Her moans rang in my ears as if she was begging me to fill her with everything I have. Sweat started beading up between us we fucked rampantly on the bed with the lights flashing across her face as she moaned. Her mouth opened and eyes closed as she gyrated her hips beneath me. She wrapped her legs around my waist and had a good grip on me.

"Hold on," I said, picking her up, still riding me and I stood holding her as she held onto my shoulders. "You good?" I asked as I started to bounce her up and down on my unit.

"Yeah," she said, biting her bottom lip. She looked at me and kissed me hard as I held her up as I glided quickly in and out of the sweet spot.

I backed up to the railing in order for her feet to touch it, giving me a bit of help in holding her and also giving her stability. She placed her feet on the top railing and bounced up and down, mouth wide open along with mine as we reached our climax together.

"Uuuuhhhh...Uuuuuuuuuhhhhh.....uuuuuuuhhhhh....fffffuuu I said as I pounded into her and filled the condom with my seed.

"Aaaaaaahhhhh......aaaaaaaaahhhhhh......fffffufuuuuuuuuuuucccc Siedah screamed and squirted against my chest as he came hard.

I felt her pussy squeeze my dick and drain it dry as it pulsated releasing her glorious nectar. I drained her. She collapsed on me. I had to quickly grab a hold of her as she laid against my chest, her arms dangling around my neck. She crossed her legs around my waist as I walked us back to the bed, kissing her slowly while squeezing her ass.

I felt myself slip out from inside her. She kissed me slowly, sucking my tongue and holding my locs as she kissed me passionately. I felt it too. I felt the connection. Unlike anyone I have ever been with.

I laid her down on the bed; she was still wrapped around me as I laid next to her pulling the duvet over us.

"You a'ight baby girl," I asked, moving her small locs behind her ear.

"Yeah, I'm good," she said, laying her head on my arm and looking at me.

• • • •

I LOOKED AT HER AND she was glowing. The lights would randomly hit her face, blue, green and red. She touched my face, tracing down my jawline down to my chin. She scooted over and kissed me on my lips slowly and softly while gazing directly at me.

"I'm hungry," she said smiling. I gave her a quick kiss. She was like no other.

She made my dick move just by hearing her passionate moans. She asks no serious questions. She asks nothing of me. No intentions just the fact we fuck really well together. I didn't think I would find a female this cool to do this. It cuts out all the drama. Justine fucked that up with me.

I can't get like that again.

"Me too, let's ride out," I said, rolling to one side of the bed as she rolled to the other side. I handed her a package of wet wipes to clean up while I threw away my filled condom.

She smiled as she got dressed after cleaning off.

"You can take a shower when we come back," I said, putting on my pants and fastening my belt.

"We're coming back?" she said stopping and smiling, putting her hand on her hip.

"Yeah," I said, pulling my shirt and grabbing my jacket. "For a midnight snack." I said smiling and walked over to her.

"Why? Are you trying to tire me out so I have to stay?" Siedah asked as she playfully pushed me. She made me smile.

"Yes."

"Why?" she asked, watching me.

I looked at her and walked over. She looked at me so sweet. Her brown eyes danced across my face as she took me in by her gaze. I touched her lips softly with my thumb and forefinger. I kissed her softly and she closed her eyes. She responded by inhaling deeply and kissing me lovingly. I parted slowly with small kisses and tipped her chin so she would look me directly in my eyes.

"So I can fuck you in the morning." I admitted.

Clearly.

Chapter 8 - Delusional

• • • •

MARCUS AND I HAVE BEEN hanging out and things are going well. He had the opportunity to work with a new rapper and he offered a few tracks that were picked up. Franklin was happy that Marcus was making moves in the business and worked with Marcus on a track with a major artist. The song got nominated for a Grammy award and now Marcus is being sought out.

I was proud of him, he was on top of his shit. It was nice to see him happy and I love that I get to share those moments with him. Marcus has been getting to me and I'm not liking it. He caters to me and makes me laugh, which makes it hard to not want to be in a relationship with him.

A relationship just creates drama because feelings are present. I feel mine growing. I get happy when I know it's the day I'm scheduled to see Marcus and I feel lost when it's not. I don't do shit when I'm alone. Monica is always with Franklin and I don't always want to be relaxing at their house.

Besides, Marcus has a lot of shit going on with Justine. She is just relentless. She showed up at another release party to which, this time, she wasn't invited.

"Monica," I said walking into the kitchen. "Justine is back,"

"What the fuck? Are you serious?" She said, turning immediately around and walked out. Monica was walking so fast I wasn't sure I was going to keep up with her.

As she rounded the corner, Justine was banging on the door, screaming and calling Marcus's name. Along with the occasional *'I see you bitch'*, pertaining to me, which she included in her rant.

"This Bitch," Monica said, opening the door. "What the fuck is wrong with you Justine? Why are you acting like this?"

"Because of that Bitch right there," she said, pointing at me. I was getting tired of being called a bitch when it wasn't endearing.

"Bitch, you know damn well, it ain't got shit to do with her," Monica said, folding her arms and looking at Justine. "Bitch you need to man the fuck up. Go home and take care of your damn kid instead of out here trying to get a man back that don't want you."

Justine looked at Monica and then looked back at me. Not many people were paying attention to the situation but there were a few who were paying attention and phones were out recording.

"Can I talk to Marcus? Please and I'll leave." she asked. I don't know the pull that Marcus has on her but I completely understand her position. He is a really good guy and very lovable. I can see how she got attached to him. But she needs to accept her consequences.

"I'll see if he'll come and talk to you, but don't expect anything." Monica said. She opened the door Justine walked in with her eyes on me. I just looked back at her trying to understand her obsession. She stood by the door and waited for Marcus to grant her wish for a moment of his time.

I followed Monica back to the living room and sat on the couch as she spoke to Marcus. He looked back at me and stared.

"I'm sorry," he said, putting his hand on my leg.

"Go ahead and handle your business." I said reassuring him. I knew they had history together and I also knew she was having a hard time losing him.

"Thanks baby girl," he said, giving me a quick peck on my lips. I smiled at him and looked at Justine. She just rolled her eyes and turned away. Marcus got up and walked over to her and both of them walked outside to talk.

Monica sat down in Marcus's place on the couch.

"Girl," she said passing me a blunt she was smoking. "That chick is fucking crazy,"

"I see," I said, taking the blunt. "She's stuck on Marcus that's for sure." I pulled on the blunt and inhaled deeply.

"Yeah," she said. "So what's up with y'all? Y'all an item now?" she asked.

"Naw, you know it's not even like that."

"Why not?"

"Justine." I said.

"What do you mean?" She said, taking back the blunt.

"She did him in. She did the ultimate. You already know how guys are when it comes to feelings."

"Yeah true," she puffed twice and passed it back. "It's hard for a guy to open back up once he's been hurt like that."

"Exactly." I pulled long and slow on the blunt. I wanted to get as high as I could to forget this part of the night. I wish it was that easy.

"But you could be the one," Monica said. I looked at her trying to figure where she was going with what she was saying.

"What do you mean?"

"You could be the one who could make him open up."

"Why are you always trying to hook me up with people?"

"Because I know how you are about relationships," she started. "I know what you went through with your Mama and Daddy. I went through it too."

"Yeah but you got Franklin."

"And you could have Marcus, if you allow yourself to open up too," she said, passing back the end of the blunt.

"Stop playing girl." I waved her off.

"I'm not playing. You know me Siedah," she said looking at me seriously. "I know you're scared, but you're not going to end up like your parents."

"But I don't want to argue and shit."

"You think Franklin and I don't argue? Shit we do almost every other day, but we work it out - *together*," she said smiling while looking at Franklin. "I don't think I would have it any other way."

I looked at Marcus as he was coming back inside alone. He looked over to me and smiled while making his way over to us.

"Besides, I see how the both of you look at each other," she said as she started standing up. "Y'all *already* got feelings for each other. Y'all are just scared to admit it." Monica quickly finished as he approached the area.

"Hey baby girl I'm back," he said as Monica passed him on her way to do her rounds as the host of the party.

"Siedah," she called before she left. "Stop waiting." Monica turned around and left.

"What are you waiting on?" Marcus asked.

"You." I said, smiling and leaning on him as he put his arm around me. It was nice to be in his arms.

We enjoyed each other a lot. We haven't had any disagreements as of yet and I wanted to keep it that way. Marcus made no indication to take our 'relationship' deeper so I wasn't going to be the one to admit that I've fallen for him. I am fine having him the way I do, at least I have him.

Marcus dropped me off at home after the party as I had to go to work in the morning. I really had to stop going to these parties during the week. Monica was used to this shit because her man has been doing it for the longest. I have not and it's showing.

· · · ·

ON ONE OF MY RANDOM errands I usually run during my lunch break, I ran into Gerald at the CVS near my job.

"Siedah," Gerald said, seeing me in the aisle. I turned and saw him walking towards me.

"Hi Gerald," I looked at him and he still looked as handsome as ever. "How are you?"

"I'm good now that I see you," he said. "How are you?"

"I'm well, thanks for asking."

"Siedah," he started. "I'm sorry I haven't contacted you all this time. I assumed we were on a break from each other."

"On a break?" I said, tilting my head and frowning a bit.

"Yeah, we had a disagreement and we took a break," he said, sounding delusional.

"Gerald," I said, looking directly at him. "We broke up. It's been over 8 months. I'm sure you've dated other women since then."

"I have, but that's because we were taking a break," he repeated.

"No. The break was us, breaking up." I said trying to get him to understand.

"No, but I didn't say it was over." *And there it goes*. The reason why I am no longer with him.

"Gerald, you don't own me." I responded.

"But we've been together." Gerald said. I knew he was not dumb as a box of rocks, but he was sure flagging down that train.

"Yes and it didn't work." I said. He looked at me as if it was finally sinking in.

"It's the other guy isn't it?" He said and I realized, it wasn't sinking in that thick ass head of his.

"Who are you talking about?"

"The guy that comes and picks you up in the black suv?"

"Are you following me?" I said questioning his sanity.

"Sometimes," He openly admitted without blinking. My eyes enlarged.

"Why?"

"Because I need you in my life," he answered.

"Gerald, you need to move on. There is no us anymore." I said, backing away to pay for my items. "And stop following me!"

"So you got someone who won't let you go too huh?" Marcus asked as we laid in the bed next to each other.

"Yeah it looks like it," I replied. I let Marcus in on my stalker, Gerald. I had to fill him in about how I think he is following me around.

"Well, you don't have to worry baby girl, ain't nobody taking you from me."

"Oh really, that's how it is?" I laid my head on his chest.

"Yeah, we have an agreement."

"True."

"Besides, you ain't trying to get back with him anyway."

"No, I am not."

"Because you are mine," he said, wrapping his arms around me and kissing my forehead.

I had driven over to the studio after work on our scheduled day. It was getting cold outside as it was getting close to Thanksgiving. It was nice laying in the bed watching the snow flurries outside the window. Marcus had changed the lights around his studio to Christmas lights which made his studio look really nice and festive. It was as if he was getting ready for a Christmas party.

We had just finished having sex and I was tired. I wasn't looking forward to getting out in the cold and driving my ass home. I was seriously reconsidering one of my stipulations of sleeping over.

"You getting tired baby girl?" He asked, nudging my nose with his.

"Yeah," I said, turning towards him. "I need to get my ass up before I get too tired to drive."

"C'mon and just stay with me," he asked, making it really hard to say no.

"I can't," I said sitting up on the side of the bed.

"Just this one time," he begged and reached for my hand. He held my hand and laced my fingers with his. "C'mon, stay."

"I can't," I said, moving to the other side of the bed. 'You're not playing fair."

"I know," he said, chuckling. "You know you want to." He was right, I did.

"I know you want me to." I retorted. I grabbed my leggings and oversized sweater to put back on.

"Yeah, I ain't gonna lie, I want you to stay. But you already know why."

"Is that the only reason?" I asked. He held his glance with me. He blushed and looked away.

"Why you asking me that? Are you going to stay if it ain't the only reason?" he asked, getting hopeful.

"It depends," I replied, trying to see where this was going.

Was Monica right? Was I able to break the barriers around Marcus's heart?

"On what?"

"On the reason." I said.

"I said because I want you to stay with me," he answered. I laughed and he joined in.

"You funny, you said that the first time you had me over here."

He laughed and shook his head. He was defeated. He knew he wanted me to stay because he had grown feelings for me, but he wasn't going to admit it. I wasn't either because I didn't want things to change between us. I didn't need what we had going on, getting ugly.

"A'ight baby girl. I'll let you go this time," he said, rolling off the bed and grabbing his shorts.

"Ah okay this time, huh? You funny." I said, grabbing my phone and my purse.

He walked me down the stairs and over to the door. Marcus helped me put my coat on before I walked out the door. He wrapped my scarf around my neck and pulled me towards him. Marcus leaned down and kissed me deeply, holding my face in hands. I held him by his waist and pulled him towards me. I loved kissing him. He was making me fall - hard.

He gave me several small kisses before stepping back and looking at me.

"Be careful and call me when you get home."

"Okay, stay back from the door so you won't get sick," I said, opening the door to leave. He kissed me quickly and I left.

On the way to my car, I noticed someone standing beside it. They were small but they watched me as I got closer holding my keys in between my fingers ready to get a punch and a stab if need be.

"Siedah," They said my name.

Who the fuck is this?

I stopped and waited for them to approach. The person walked slowly towards me and the street light hit their face - *it was Justine!* Not this bitch again.

"Justine?" I asked, trying to figure out what she was doing there and how long she was waiting.

I ain't got time to be dealing with this type of drama. This bitch is psychotic.

"So you with him now?" Justine asked.

"Why does it matter? Are you being serious?"

"Yes, I'm serious!" Justine said, stepping towards me. I stepped back, as I wasn't sure if she had something in her pockets or not.

"Why?"

"Because he's my man!" She screamed. This bitch is delusional too.

"Is he though? Is he your son's father?"

Reality Check! I know it was harsh but somebody had to.

"Leave my son out of this! Bitch, you don't know me!" she said, stepping closer to me.

"You're right, I don't know you. I just know what I've been told. But if any of it's true, then be a woman and save face. Ok, you fucked up. Own that shit. We've all fucked up one time or another. Shit, some of us is still fucking up. But you got a *kid*. Think about *him*. Make sure he doesn't end up doing the same shit we doing."

"How would you know?"

"Because I'm woman enough to own my own fuck ups and sometimes they come with deep regrets. That's how I know." I responded.

Justine looks at me for a long time. I wasn't sure if she was about to attack me or not but I was on guard until she lowered her gaze and scoffs, shook her head and then slowly backed away walking off down the street.

I watched her disappear down the street; a pair of headlights made a u-turn at the end of the block.

I couldn't wait to get in the car and tell Monica this shit.

Chapter 9 - Admissions Made

Siedah

Things had quieted down for a while and I thought we were in the clear of interruptions from the exes. Apparently, mine wouldn't go away quietly. Gerald had been calling and texting me randomly and frequently since I had last seen him in CVS. I finally got fed up with him and decided to put the point across that I was not coming back to him.

"Gerald, it's over between us. You need to move on, seriously." I said to him over the phone. I could hear him exhaling. He did not like my response.

"Siedah, I understand we had a break, but you know we can do this," he replied.

"There is no we, Gerald. I've moved on and you should too," I said. I didn't want to bring up Marcus because we weren't in a relationship but he needed to know that I was fucking someone else on a regular basis.

"So it is that nigga?" he stated. "Why do you like that thug ass nigga?"

"He ain't a thug ass nigga! Right now you being the thug ass nigga, nigga!" I got loud, forgetting I was at work. I stood up and glanced around. Todd looked at me along with a few others. I just shook my head and left the office to go to the breakroom.

"Siedah don't do this to me," he pleaded. "Let me come see you."

"No. I don't want to see you Gerald. I am not doing this to you, you are doing this all by yourself," I didn't know how else to tell him. He needed to get it in his motherfucking head that *he* was the root of all of this shit brewing in his mind.

"What does that nigga have that I don't have?" Gerald said.

Fuck it. I went in on a nigga.

"Sense," I boldly stated. The silence on the other side of the phone had me thinking he had hung up on me. I heard cars driving in the background which meant he was still holding the phone trying to find a good comeback.

I have a slick tongue sometimes. When I'm at that point - I'll get you off of me.

"Why does it have to be him Siedah?" he asked. "He ain't doing shit with his life, probably smoking weed all day and fucking bitches. You're better than that Siedah!" he yelled.

Yes, Gerald was bougie too. Fine as fuck and the sex is absolutely amazing, I damn near cried one time. But it's his mind games he plays and the demands he has that I couldn't handle. He's like one of these brothas that got out the ghetto and is trying to forget where he came from yet being a proud black man in the financial industry. Gerald felt like people who don't work in 'certified' or 'degreed' careers were beneath him.

He was fucked up in his thinking.

"Ain't nothing wrong with weed Gerald, you used to smoke it with me." I said.

"Only with you have I ever smoked weed, you see, this is why I need you."

"So you can smoke weed? Gerald, you can just buy some, its legal here." I said fucking with him. I've learned well at playing those mind games with him.

I'm a fucking pro.

"Siedah," he said, sounding serious. "I see that I'm going to have to deal with someone then."

The hairs on the back of my neck stood up instantly. I didn't like the sound of that. "What are you talking about Gerald?"

"You'll find out. I'll call you later. I have to take care of the situation." He said, hanging up.

What was this motherfucker up to?

Thanksgiving came and went with Christmas on the way. Marcus kind of got his Christmas gift early with the Grammy nomination, but I wanted to get him something special. Of course Monica and Franklin were having a Christmas party on the Saturday before Christmas which I figured I would give Marcus the gift of me staying over after the party.

When Marcus and I arrived at the party, it was already in full swing. Monica had informed me that Justine was coming but she said she wasn't staying for long.

"Why is she coming?" I asked.

"The girl may be a bit crazy, but she's a friend and a good singer. Franklin wanted to put down all the fighting for Christmas. He told her if she acted a fool, she would be done." she said.

"Well, I ain't trippin. I just don't want her to spoil the party for everyone."

"Oh naw, she ain't, She ain't staying long, she'll have her son with her. She said she wanted to stop by and give Franklin and I gifts. She said she's on her way to be with her people in Atlanta." Monica finished.

"Oh ok, well that's good." I was happy Justine had calmed down. I guess after our little conversation outside of Marcus's place did some good. It could have been like that a long time ago.

"Yeah, I'm saying," Monica took a sip of her drink. "So how's Psycho Asshole?"

"I haven't heard from him since that phone call," I said. I had to tell Monica about the phone call I had with Gerald.

I wasn't sure if I should tell Marcus because I knew Gerald was delusional but he usually kept himself together. Besides he was always worried about his job and position and shit so I figured he wouldn't jeopardize that shit by doing something crazy.

"Well that was a few weeks ago, so maybe he finally got the hint?" she quipped.

"I hope so."

Marcus came and sat next to me on the couch.He was smiling and enjoying himself. Everyone was still congratulating him on the grammy nomination. He was happy his name was getting out there and getting noticed for his music. That's what he's wanted and it couldn't come at a better time.

"I'm gonna go and get a beer, you want one?" I asked Marcus.

"Yeah baby girl, thanks," he said as I stood up and rubbed my booty. He smiled at me and winked. This man was amazing.

He has been the perfect gentleman. He was straight up serious about just being with each other. I've seen other females try to slide up on him when I'm not in the vicinity. He immediately tells them he's not interested.

"Siedah," Franklin said as I entered the kitchen. "Merry Christmas."

"Merry Christmas Franklin." I replied, giving him a hug.

"You know, I'm glad you and my boy got together."

"Well you know we ain't really together, right?"

"I don't care what y'all call it, y'all together shit," he said, taking a swig of his beer. He helped me open two Heineken. "That nigga is in love again," he finished. I looked at him as he handed me back the beers.

"What?" I asked. I was sure I didn't hear him correctly.

"I said, that nigga in love with you." he repeated looking at me and raising his eyebrows. My stomach fluttered. Marcus was in love with me.

"And how do you know that?" I said, pursing up my lips and adjusting my weight to one side.

"'Cause I know that nigga. He was like this with Justine, but it's different this time. He seems happier, and the nigga can't stop talking about you." Franklin said taking another swig of his beer.

I followed suit and took a swig of one of the beers I was holding. "He ain't tell me nothing."

"And, he's not going to until he knows how you feel first," he said. I looked at Franklin and he smiled. "I can see, you in love with him too."

"How do you know that?" I asked my heart was pounding in my chest.

Was I that transparent?

"Just by the way you answered," he smiled. "If you weren't in love with him you would've said that you weren't. But you didn't, did you?" Franklin had called me out. I smiled and looked down. He leaned down to keep eye contact and we both laughed.

"Shut up you don't know nothing." I said smiling.

"I know you and I know him. Y'all should get together, it'll be nice to have my best friend and his girl with me and Monica. Besides you are already Monica's best friend so it's inevitable," he said, drinking the last of his beer.

"We'll see." I said as I left the kitchen.

Monica

. . . .

SIEDAH HAD LEFT TO grab some drinks which gave me the perfect time to ask Marcus what up with them.

"Marcus," I said as I turned to him on the couch. He was rolling up a nice, fat ass blunt at the table.

"Wassup Monica," he said, adding more ganja to an already full blunt wrapper.

"That's what I'm tryin' to find out. What's up with you and Siedah?" I said. He smiled and wouldn't look at me.

"I don't know what you talkin' 'bout," He gave me a sly grin.

"You know what the fuck I'm talkin' 'bout," I said bumping him slightly making some if the ganja fall out of the wrapper. We both laughed. "My bad. For real though, I know you Marcus and I know Siedah."

"I know." he said, fixing the blunt and finishing it up.

"You fell for her didn't you," I asked. He didn't say anything which was a clear indication that he did.

"I don't know what...,"

"Yes you do nigga, don't play with me." I bumped him again and he chuckled.

"Did Franklin put you up to this?"

"Naw, why?"

"'Cause we had a similar talk earlier today."

"Probably because we were talking about you and Siedah finally getting *together*- together," I replied.

"I know," He lit the end. "Siedah is the shit, I must admit."

"She got you fallin' don't she?" He looked at me and smiled. He closed his eyes and shook his head.

"Yeah she does," he admitted.

"I knew it!" I said, getting excited. He laughed and shook his head. "So what are you gonna do about it ?"

"I really haven't thought about it really. I know I got a thing for her though." He admitted.

"I knew she would break through that wall you put up after Justine."

"Yeah, she did. I guess it was how she handled all of it. She didn't ask me anything. She ain't needy. She does her own shit and makes time for me when we get together."

"Yup, that's my girl."

"Yeah, but is she gonna stay that way?" Marcus wondered. I knew he had his doubts with good reason given his track record with Justine.

"I know what you're saying and worried about, but Siedah ain't like that. She's just as scared as you are. She's just like me, a product of divorce. So she's just being careful because she doesn't want to end up like her parents." I said.

"I feel you. She won't have to worry about that Monica, you know me." He was being sincere.

"I know, that's why I wanted y'all to meet. Shit, I think I've found my calling - Matchmaker." I said seriously thinking about it.

"Monica, your ass is crazy." Marcus chuckled.

"Well I know I got skills because I got y'all together. Have I ever asked you to hook up with someone else?" I said knowing I had a point.

"You right, you haven't. And you did good this time," he said looking at Siedah as she returned with two beers.

"Hey girl," I said as she passed Marcus a beer. "Have you seen Franklin?" I said changing the subject.

"Yeah, he's in the kitchen. That was the last place I saw him." She said pointing towards the kitchen.

"Ok cool," I moved out of the way so Siedah could sit down next to Marcus. "I'm out y'all." I said leaving the living room to find Franklin.

Marcus

• • • •

"HEY BABY GIRL," SIEDAH had returned with beers and sat down next to me. I leaned over and gave her a quick kiss.

"Hey babe," she replied. I loved that she called me 'babe'. I guess Monica was right, she has broken my barrier.

I wanted to confess it to her but I don't want it to end up like it did with Justine. I know Siedah is nothing like Justine, it's just that I didn't know Justine was like she was either until shit happened. But Monica reassured me that Siedah wasn't like that at all. And I believe her. I like what we have going on for real, it's just natural and real. I can tell she cares for me.

"Are you ready for your gifts?" I said picking up a gift bag from underneath the table.

"You said gifts?"

"Yeah, I got you more than one." Siedah smiled like a little kid. She loved Christmas, I could tell.

"Well I have one for you now and another for you later," she said leaning in and placing a kiss on my lips. Siedah made it easy to fall in love with her. She never asked for anything and

I don't think she would. She is just down to earth and honest and that's what I love about her.

"Oooo, okay I can't wait," I said smiling. She smiled back at me as she passed me a box.

"Thank you baby girl."

Siedah just had a way of making me smile and I loved the way she looked at me. She looked like she loved me open heartedly. She didn't have drama, aside from the dude following her. But it's been a while since she has mentioned him so I figured she handled it.

I unwrapped the gift to reveal a red box. I knew exactly what it was. It was a watch from an Instagram influencer who sold his watches online. It was a Hagley North watch. It was the watch I told her I wanted. Siedah listened to me and got something I wanted.

I absolutely loved this woman.

"Oh babe, for real!" I said, getting excited. "Are you serious?"

"I knew you wanted it. I pay attention," she smiled. She was happy that I loved the gift, she was smiling hard. Franklin leaned over the couch to take a look.

"That shit is nice, It's from the guy on the internet right?"

"Yeah," she responded.

"Is that from the guy that goes *live* in people's cities and then people gotta find him right?"

"Yup, that's him," I replied, putting on the watch.

"That shit is tight," Franklin said, nodding in approval.

"I'm glad you like it," She grinned. It fit perfectly. I leaned over and planted a nice, long kiss on her lips.

"Hey y'all can go to the room for all that shit," Monica said as she passed us following Franklin.

We laughed and I passed her the gift bag.

"Thank you babe," Siedah said as she excitedly took the bag.

She pulled out three small jewelry boxes. One had a pair of diamond earrings, another had a matching diamond tennis bracelet and the last was a diamond necklace. She looked blown away by the gifts so much she teared up.

"Thank you baby!" she said, giving me a tight hug. She deserved it all. I must admit, she had my heart. She had made it through all of the bullshit.

"Merry Christmas baby girl," I said, kissing her cheek repeatedly.

"Merry Christmas baby," she said softly.

Chapter 10 - Choices Revealed

SIEDAH

The Christmas Party was off the chain. I had a blast and I was happy that I got to share it with my favorite people - Monica, Franklin and Marcus. I was so happy I was with Marcus. I must admit, he had me hooked. I can see how Justine didn't want to give this up. I don't want to either.

Marcus and I were on our way back to his spot when I decided to tell him about his second gift.

"So, Marcus," I reached over to hold his hand. He laced his fingers with mine and kissed the back of my hand while keeping his eyes on the road.

"Wassup baby girl?"

"I wanna play some music," I said, searching for the song on the display. "I found it," I played Drake & J.Cole, _In the Morning._

"That's the shit," he said as held my hand.

"Well why don't we see what he is talking about?" I asked, leaning towards him in the seat.

"What you mean?" He was focused on driving. I didn't want to distract him by playing around so I just let it out.

"Fucking in the morning," I said. A smile spread across his face.

"You serious?" he asked, glancing periodically at me trying to keep his eyes on the road.

"Yup, I'm serious." Marcus smiled hard and kissed the back of my hand again.

"Aww shit yeah," he said. "That's what I'm talkin' 'bout baby girl." .

Shortly after I gave him my second gift, we arrived at his place. The snow flurries were in full swing as the wind was swirling flakes all around. We had a few gifts in the backseat that we needed to get and I wanted to grab them as quickly as possible to eliminate me being outside in the fucking cold for too long.

Marcus came around and helped me out the suv and then opened the back door to grab the bags.

"Don't forget the little bag on the seat, that's your watch," I said as I saw him collecting the bags.

"We got a lot of shit."

"I know, I feel like a kid at Christmas," I said looking up as the snowflakes fell quickly from the sky. I heard a car door close and I looked to see where as I didn't notice anyone driving down the street.

I saw a tall manly figure walk towards us from across the street. When the figure reached the middle of the street the light hit his face - It was Gerald! I was shocked as I saw him walking quickly as he raised his arm towards us. He had a gun!

"Noooo!" I screamed pushing the door closed on Marcus in the back seat while holding up my hands to block anything.

POW!

I heard a gunshot. It was loud as fuck.

I felt instant pain. I wasn't feeling well anymore. I grabbed my chest and my legs collapsed underneath me.

The snow on the ground was cold as my face lay in a deep blanket of flakes.

I heard Marcus scream my name.

• • • •

POW! POW!

Two more shots. My vision was blurry as I saw Gerald standing over Marcus.

"Marcus!" I struggled to speak. "Noo!"

I was fading out. It was so cold.

I closed my eyes. I didn't want to see it.

• • • •

POW! Another shot. I can't hold on.

• • • •

I DON'T WANT TO.

• • • •

I'M SORRY MARCUS.

• • • •

MARCUS

Siedah had just told me that she was staying the night. Something I had been waiting on since I met her. She is something special to me and I don't want to lose her. I can honestly admit that to myself for once that I have found real love again.

As I got the gifts out the back, suddenly Siedah screamed and I heard a gunshot. I turned around to see who was shooting and I see Siedah on the ground and some nigga standing in the middle of the street.

"Siedah!" I yelled as I went to her.

POW! POW!

I heard two gunshots which blew me back against the suv. I instantly fell to the ground.

I saw Siedah on the ground barely moving. She was trying to reach out to me.

I couldn't get to my baby. My chest was on fire. This nigga shot me twice.

I saw him approach us, walking my way. I started fading out. I needed to get to Siedah.

I hear footsteps from behind me.

POW! Another shot.

Everything went black.

• • • •

MONICA

• • • •

I WAS GETTING TIRED and the party had finally ended. This was one of the best Christmas parties we've ever had. Marcus and Siedah were in love and I was happy. They looked so good together. Franklin told me that Siedah was in love with Marcus from the talk they had in the kitchen earlier. I knew she would fall for him. Franklin knew that Siedah would be the one to be able to make Marcus happy again. I had to give it to him as he suggested the two get together first.

• • • •

MY PHONE RANG WITH a number that I didn't recognize. It read *Stroger Hospital - Emergency*.

I just knew this was a wrong number.

"Hello?" I answered, getting ready to tell them they had reached the wrong number.

"Is this Monica Brown?" The female voice said over the phone.

"Yes?"

"Do you know Siedah Jackson?" she asked. My heart started pounding.

"Yes," I started breathing faster. "What happened?"

"She's been shot," she said and I went numb. Not Siedah. She was just here. I hear Franklin yell for me from the kitchen.

"Monica!!" He yelled, running to the living room. I looked at him and he looked lost. "Marcus got shot!" he said, holding a phone to his ear.

"Siedah did too!" I screamed. Tears started falling down my face. This shit cannot be happening right now.

"Let's ride out to the hospital," Franklin said, holding out his hand. We were out the door and headed over.

There wasn't a lot of traffic so we got to the hospital in a reasonable amount of time considering it was winter in Chicago. Franklin parked in the emergency parking lot and we ran in the entrance.

"Excuse me, we had a call about our family that were here," I said as I reached the triage desk.

"One moment," the nurse said behind the desk. She typed on a computer and then looked back at me. "What's the name sweetheart?"

"Siedah Jackson,"

"And Marus Harper," Franklin chimed in. He was pacing back and forth trying to maintain control.

"Everything's going to be okay," I said out loud. "Right?" I looked at Franklin for reassurance.

He just grabbed me tightly while I broke down. I was tired of being strong.

• • • •

MORE THAN AN HOUR HAD passed before we got to see either one of them. The police had shown up and were asking questions. But we had nothing to go on.

"Thank you for meeting with us," Officer #1 said. I didn't even bother to remember them because I wanted to find out about Siedah.

"What happened?" I asked sitting next to Franklin in a private waiting room.

"That's where we were hoping you would give us some insight," he responded.

"Shit we know just as much as y'all know!" Franklin said, getting upset. "They just left our house. We had a Christmas party and they just left,"

"Did they get into any altercations with anyone at the party?" Officer #2 asked.

"No, nothing happened. It was a cordial party, we don't play that shit." I chimed in. My head was banging with the worst headache ever.

"Do you know of anyone who they had an issue with?" He asked. "Someone who may want to harm them?"

"Naw, not really." I said and then I thought about Psycho Asshole. "Psycho Asshole!" I yelled and smacked my leg.

"What?" Franklin said, turning towards Monica.

"Psycho Asshole! I bet it was that motherfucker!" I said pointing at Franklin.

"Who is this Ma'am?" Officer #1 asked leaning in.

"Shit, I knew she should have said something about him to Marcus." I said. I covered my mouth.

"You mean dude following Siedah?" Franklin said.

"Yeah that motherfucker." I looked at him and tears started falling.

"Who is this guy?" The officer asked again.

"Um...he's...uh..Siedah's ex boyfriend. His name is Gerald, but I don't know his last name," Franklin said while consoling me. I was losing it. I bet it was that motherfucker. Siedah told me about that phone call.

"Would his name be Gerald Greene?" he asked. I looked up. That was his name. Gerald Greene.

"Yes, Yes, yes. That motherfucker! He did it! I know he did," I cried. I just needed to see her. My best friend. My sister. My road dog.

"How do you know he did it?" The officer asked.

"Uh...Siedah told Monica Gerald called her one day and threatened her because she was seeing Marcus," Franklin stammered out. He was trying to keep it together for me because I was losing it all over the place.

"Ok. Thank you for that," Officer #1 replied.

"So y'all need to catch that motherfucker and you got the one who did all this shit!" I screamed. I started crying harder. I just wanted my friend.

"Could you tell me if either Siedah or Marcus carried a weapon?" Officer #2 asked.

"No....,neither one of them, why?" Franklin asked as I tried to get myself together.

"Well, we found Gerald Greene dead at the scene," he said.

My skin turned cold and instantly filled with goosebumps. He was dead. Gerald was dead.

"How?" I was trying to make sense of all of this shit that was happening all at once.

"He was shot in the head," he answered. "We found him not far from your friends."

"What a fucking way to die." I shook my head. "God don't like ugly."

Chapter 11 - Christmas Present

MONICA

• • • •

THAT WAS A LOT OF SHIT to try and process. I thought I was having the best Christmas this year, as everybody was getting along. We were growing in the business and things had just started happening for us. Marcus and Siedah had just gotten together and this shit had to happen. Gerald's stupid ass had to go and fuck our entire world up.

• • • •

"SO HE SHOT HIMSELF?" I asked. This motherfucker took the easy way out.

"It looks like it," The officer said. "We'll find out more once we get the ballistics back on the bullets."

"Oh," I didn't have anything else to say because that motherfucker did it. The officers left and Franklin and I were still in the private waiting area trying to make sense of all of this shit.

"This is going to be one fucked up Christmas," Franklin said, sitting back in the chair. Our phones had been blowing up because this shit hit the news.

We knew it would because shit doesn't stay quiet in Chicago. Before we knew it our phones were being bombarded by news outlets trying to get the scoop on Marcus because he was a Grammy nominated producer who got shot going home late at night.

Social media had created their own story about Marcus having an affair and Siedah's boyfriend found out. This shit got crazy, fast. I know they say that even bad press is good press. *But is it though?* This shit was getting out of hand.

· · · ·

FRANKLIN AND I HAD been in the hospital going on about 3 hrs before someone pulled us aside to talk.

"Hi," A middle aged black woman who looked like she was a MILF, pulled us to the side and gave us the details. "I'm Nurse Brown, I'm taking care of Siedah Jackson. I heard you are here to see her, correct?"

"Yes! Yes, please......Thank you...thank...," I burst into tears. Siedah was still alive. No one told us anything, We were in limbo just waiting yet answering questions when asked.

"It's okay baby," she said, patting me on my arm. "Come with me," she said and I followed, Franklin not far behind.

"Do you know anything about Marcus Harper?" Franklin asked as we walked down the corridor to a room.

"Naw, but you might be able to find out at the Nurse's station," she pointed towards where we just came. "But she's in there." she said walking off.

I walked in the room and tears started falling. There were machines and lines and oxygen everywhere. My friend was alive, but sleeping. She made no movement, no reaction to us walking in the room. I covered my mouth as I saw a bandage wrapped around her chest. She had a breathing tube in her mouth and a monitor for her heart.

"Franklin," I said looking at my friend. "She....," I couldn't believe all of this happened just a few minutes after they left the party.

"She's alive Monica," he said, grabbing me. "She's alive. Everything is going to be alright," he consoled me. He was scared too. I heard him sniff and wipe away tears. He was hurting too. I wrapped my arms around him and hugged him tight.

"Thank God," I said. "You need to go and check on Marcus." I said, tapping him on the shoulder. "I'm gonna sit right here."

I pointed to the chair right next to her bed. I wanted to be there when she woke up. I wanted to be the first face she saw when she opened her eyes.

"Ok I'll be back," Franklin said leaving the room.

• • • •

I SAT THERE LOOKING at Siedah, hoping and praying she would open her eyes, just once and tell me she was okay. My phone kept blowing up to the point I had to make a statement. I told Franklin I would handle the press while he tried to find Marcus. I sent a statement stating that Marcus was out with a female friend when they both got ambushed.

That quieted the media down for a minute while I focused on Siedah. I called her mother and let her know. She said she would come up as soon as she can since she relocated to Atlanta. Franklin came back into the room after getting news on Marcus.

"He's here, but in intensive care," he said trying to hold up from breaking down. Marcus was like his brother with Franklin being an only child. I ran over and grabbed him as he cried. I only heard Franklin cry one other time before, when his mother died. This sounded just like that kind of cry.

"It's going to be okay baby, I promise." I said, unsure myself. I had to be strong for the both of us.

• • • •

IT WAS DAY 2 WHEN SIEDAH woke up - *Christmas Day*. I guess it was going to be a semi-good Christmas, Marcus was still in intensive care with no improvement. I was there when Siedah started frailing all over trying to get the tube out of her throat.

"Wait! Wait Bitch," I said, grabbing her hands as she was trying to pull her breathing tube out. "Let me call the nurse," I said, showing her and pushing the button.

The nurse came in quickly into the room.

"Yes?"

"She's awake and trying to take this fucking tube out her mouth." I said looking at her, smoothing her locs back and smiling. "I love you girl, I'm so happy you woke up," I leaned down and whispered in her ear. The nurse left to get assistance to remove the tube.

Tears started streaming down the sides of her face. I started crying too. I was smiling but still crying. I was so happy to see her looking back at me. She was going to be okay. I couldn't tell her about Marcus, not right now. She just came back to me. That will have to wait.

By the end of the day Siedah had the tube removed and was laying in the bed talking softly. Flowers flooded her room from Marcus's followers and Franklin's as well. Siedah's name was leaked by that face recognition shit. Someone from who attended a past party provided pictures and video of them cozying up on the couch. Everyone was sending prayers for a quick recovery.

Everybody loved them, because they were good people. They were down to earth people who treated everyone the same. Siedah and Marcus weren't about the bullshit and the drama, they were about living life and having a good time with like-minded people. They liked to have a good time with everybody and everyone realized they were together - even though they would say different.

They belonged together.

. . . .

"HOW'RE YOU FEELING?" I asked as she turned her head towards me. Siedah held out her hand and I grabbed and held it.

"I'm here," she spoke softly. "I feel like shit," she said holding her stomach.

"You look like shit too, the hospital gown does nothing for you." I joked trying to make light of the situation. I'm a wreck when serious shit happens. Siedah smiled and shook her head.

"How long have you been here?"

"Since it happened Boo," I said, wiping away random tears falling from my eyes.

"It was Gerald," she said, straining to talk louder. "It was Gerald. That motherfucker...,"

"We know Sweetie," I said, trying to calm her down. She was getting upset and started crying, probably reliving the incident. She saw him shoot her.

"It was Gerald!" she softly screamed. I stood up and tried to hug her in between all the tubes and shit attached to her. "Did they find him?"

"Yes girl, they found him," I answered. "He was found dead not too far from you and Marcus. The police think it was suicide." I informed her. Siedah looked stunned. She stared at me as I wasn't telling the truth.

It wasn't until she realized I had no other comeback that I was speaking facts.

"Dead?"

"Yup, he shot himself in the head." I said. She laid her head back and looked around the room taking in the information.

"Marcus! Where's Marcus?" she asked, getting flustered again.

"Calm down Siedah," I said as monitors were beeping faster the more she got upset.

"Where is Marcus?" Siedah asked again, holding my hand, begging me to tell her. I didn't want to tell her that he took bullets to the chest. I was still trying to deal with the one she took to the chest.

"I can't." Tears started falling steadily. She looked at me and covered her mouth and closed her eyes. Tears started streaming down her face the harder she cried. Franklin walked in the room just at the right time.

"Siedah, you're awake," he said, walking over to the bed. He looked at me and then at Siedah. "How you feeling?"

"Marcus," she spoke to Franklin. "What happened?" Franklin adjusted himself as he stood by the bed trying to figure out how to tell her. He looked at me and I was crying.

"Gerald must have followed y'all one day in order to find out where Marcus stayed." He started. I could tell it was hard for him as he pulled over a chair to sit down to finish.

"He followed us. He was already parked when we got to the studio," she whispered.

"You should tell that to the police. Now that you're awake they will probably want to know," I said.

"I saw him shoot me," she said and both Franklin and I remained quiet. We couldn't even imagine what they went through that day.

"Well Gerald shot you and then shot Marcus twice in the chest," Franklin said. Siedah covered her mouth and cried hard. I tried to calm her down by wiping her tears and smoothing her locs back. I wanted to grab and hold her and I couldn't

"Did he make it? Please tell me he made it! Please Franklin….oh….please….," she said trailing off and crying harder.

"Siedah, calm down," I said, trying to get her to gain her composure.

"Yeah, he made it. But barely, he's in intensive care. He ain't woken up yet though." Franklin said lowering his head. He didn't like seeing Marcus with all the medical shit going on just like I didn't like seeing Siedah the same way.

"Oh Thank God! My baby is still here," she said. I knew she loved him. She would have been devastated if he didn't make it.

"He'll be fine, he just needs to recover," Franklin said. "Both of y'all had immediate surgery, but with him taking two slugs to the chest, there was a bit more damage."

"How bad is he?" she asked.

"Collapsed lung and severed spleen I think they said. Luckily, the bullets missed major organs,"

"Thank God!" I said, getting a little relief. I might not be the most church going person but I know who rules the universe and I have to give Him praises when shit like this happens and the people I love are still able to be here.

"Oh my goodness." Siedah said. She just looked lost trying to process all of the information. She's been through a lot and all she was worried about is Marcus.

"It's all good girl, y'all still here. I love you girl, I thought I lost you." I said as I put my head on her hand. She smoothed down my locs as she tried to calm me.

"I love you too girl. Thank you for being here for me, both of y'all,"

"Y'all family Siedah, we had to come." Franklin stated.

He was right, we were family.

Chapter 12 - New Years Resolution

MONICA

. . . .

I WENT TO SEE SIEDAH every day, I wanted to see her to make sure she was coming back to me. Her mother finally came up and we would take breaks on being there with her in the hospital. I still had to help Franklin. Life still went on outside the hospital.

On day 5 they had Siedah get up and walk around the hospital corridor outside her room. She was in a lot of pain getting off the bed, but she was determined. I was able to walk her up and down the hallways.

"How you doing, girl?" I asked as she slowly walked, taking each step carefully while dragging along her fluids. She had her other hand wrapped in my arm for balance.

"I'm doing, shit," she said, stepping slowly. She paused and took a breath. "I wanna see Marcus." she panted as she took another step.

"I know you do Boo, but let's get you up and running first so you can help him," I responded. I knew she wanted to see him. But he's still messed up, trying to recover. I just know he's gonna make it.

He has to. For Siedah.

"I know," she said as she took another step. "I just need to see him. He needs to hear my voice," she finished.

"I know Siedah, and you will," I said, reassuring her. "Let's work on you first." And we continued up and down the hallway.

"It's crazy that Gerald did all of this." Siedah uttered. I could hear the regretful tone in her voice.

"He was obsessed with you and he didn't want anyone else to have you," We stepped slowly, wavering back and forth like an old couple.

"But he had so much going on. He had a great life with the ideal job and he was growing as an individual in the financial world. But he wanted me," she mentioned. She didn't understand why Gerald couldn't leave her alone. .

"You are an amazing person Siedah," I tapped her hand as she held on to me.

"I know I'm amazing, that's why you're my sistah-girlfriend," she joked as we made a u-turn at the end of the hallway.

"Oh you got jokes, okay well you comin' back," I laughed.

I was happy my Siedah was coming back.

Siedah

Here I was, in the hospital. Gerald had shot me over some shit that I probably pushed him to do. But he also shot Marcus too. He didn't deserve it. He didn't have to deal with my bullshit. I didn't want him to get hurt at all. At least Justine just cheated on him, I got this motherfucker *shot*.

"I can't believe he shot himself though, that's some sick shit to just kill yourself," I couldn't understand the *'why'* behind it all.

. . . .

"YEAH IT IS, JUST TO finish your life right there - The End." Monica said.

. . . .

IT MADE ME THINK. MONICA was right.

. . . .

HE ENDED HIS LIFE BECAUSE he couldn't have me.

. . . .

"DO YOU THINK MARCUS will be mad?" I asked.

. . . .

"MAD? WHY WOULD HE BE mad at you?"

. . . .

"BECAUSE OF WHAT HAPPENED," I said as I stopped as we headed back to my room. I had had enough of walking. "I didn't want him to get hurt because of me,"

"Girl please, he is not going to be mad at you." Monica said as we stopped at the door.

"Bitch I got him shot!" I whispered loudly.

"Bitch, no you didn't. Gerald bitch ass shot Marcus!" Monica huffed.

"Yeah because of me!" Raising my voice a bit made my chest hurt. I walked slowly over to the bed and Monica helped me scoot to the middle of the bed.

"No, Gerald shot him because he was delusional. Not because of you, that was on him," she said, getting upset.

"You know what I mean though," I said, adjusting the pillow. "Do you think that he would be upset?"

"No girl, he loves you. That I know," she said smiling and sticking her tongue out. She made me smile.

Marcus loved me. I just needed to see him. I wanted him to know that I didn't mean for all of this shit to happen. I wouldn't wish this on my worst enemy. I smiled as I thought about him. I pulled out my phone and looked at the pictures we took of each other when we went out to eat. I loved taking pictures of my food so every chance I got, I would take a picture and post it on my Instagram account.

I incorporated Marcus in my insta photos when I took a picture of his massive burrito he ordered from the Mexican place. I had a few pictures of him smiling with his burrito as he took bites. As I kept scrolling I came upon the pictures from the Grammy nomination party. He looked so handsome.

I wanted to see his face up close. I wanted to hear him breathing. I wanted to see him lick his bottom lip.

As I kept going, I reached the Christmas pictures. We looked so happy. We looked like we were in love. Monica caught us under the mistletoe and she took a picture as we kissed. We belonged together and I hoped he wouldn't hate me after this. I didn't know Gerald was unstable, had I known I wouldn't have watched my mouth.

I froze as I saw the last picture we took together; we were inside the car. We had just pulled up and he said Merry Christmas to me again. He was happy that I was staying over.

We never got to that part.

• • • •

FRANKLIN

• • • •

I CAN'T STAND SEEING Marcus like this. This is hard for me. I've been trying to stay strong for Monica, it's gotten better since Siedah woke up, but I need Marcus to wake up now. I pushed open the door to the ICU and walked to his room. He was still the same, oxygen breathing for him, heart monitor beeping and Marcus just laying there without a clue as to where he was.

"Hey Marcus," I said, pulling over a chair to the side of the bed. "I'm back man," I looked at him and he didn't move. His eyes fluttered a bit but they have been doing that for the past two days. The nurse said that it's just a reaction.

"Hey man, you gotta wake up brah. I need you man. You got the Grammys nigga, we gotta do that together brah," I spoke standing over him. A monitor alarm rang off and scared the shit out of me. A nurse rushed in and checked the monitor and turned it off and rushed back out the room. I looked at the monitor like I knew what the hell it was and she rushed back in with a bag of liquid.

"His fluids are out, gotta keep him hydrated," she said, replacing the bag and restarting the monitor.

"Come on man, wake up," I sat down, leaning my head on the side of the bed. "Siedah wants to see you, man. Wake up for her, she needs you man," I said as I sat beside him talking to him, hoping he would hear my voice. I remembered that's what they always say in the movies so I decided to try it. Anything is possible.

"Everybody is waiting for you and Siedah to get out of the hospital so y'all can be home to recover. Siedah just got out of bed today. She's getting back on her feet man, for you,"

I said while my eyes started tearing up. "So you gotta get back on your feet for her man, please."

I missed my boy. Marcus is my nigga. He's been there for me since we met all those years ago. It's hard to see him lying up in the hospital over dumb shit. Some nigga couldn't let Siedah go and decided to try to end both of their lives. He didn't think all the way through. He didn't wait around to see if they lived or died.

To be honest, I'm glad he didn't stick around, because he probably would've finished them off and I wouldn't even be talking to Marcus right now. It's just fucked up. It fucked up Christmas and now New Years is gonna be fucked up too. It's too late to cancel the party due it being a promotional event as well, shareholders will be present so that's something we can't just cancel.

"Brah, you need to wake your ass up before New Years, 'cause I don't want to start off the New Years like this shit," I said looking at him. His hand shook a bit, his leg jerked and his eyes fluttered again. Reactions. That's what the nurse said. If it is, he needs to react to me talking to his ass.

I leaned down to his ear and whispered, "You need to wake your bitch ass up, nigga. Siedah is waiting for you and so am I." I said standing up straight. I gave him a "pound" on his hand and left.

I'll be back tomorrow. I've had enough for today.

Franklin

. . . .

NEW YEAR'S EVE HAD come and I wanted to see Marcus before the day got too busy. Monica and I had the New Years Eve Bash and we wouldn't be able to come to the hospital for New Years anyway so I came early to see Siedah and Marcus. I stopped by Siedah's room first and she had family members stop by which kept her busy.

"Are you coming back before you leave?" she asked. Siedah looked a lot better. She still said she was in a bit of pain and she felt a lot better.

"Yeah, I'll stop by before I leave," I smiled and I backed out of her room.

I walked over to damn near what seemed like the other side of the hospital, to the ICU. All the nurses and doctors were festive and getting ready for their work shift for New Years. I walked into Marcus' room and it was decorated for the new year aside from the flowers and gifts from his fans.

"Hey man, I'm back. I came early because of the party," I said as I pulled up the chair to the side of the bed.

"I wish you could be there, man. Shit, I wish both you and Siedah could be there," I said looking at him. His eyes started fluttering again like before. "I wish you would open your fucking eyes man, just wake the fuck up!" I said out loud. I was getting frustrated that my boy wasn't awake. I was happy he was here but he wasn't here.

I just looked at him, eyes fluttering and moving; and then it happened - he opened his eyes! I saw his eyes open but I wasn't sure I was seeing what I was seeing. He was staring straight up to the ceiling which was inevitable with him laying on his back. His eyes moved to one side of the room and then towards the other side, which is where I was.

"Marcus!" I said as I stood up. He looked at me, with the breathing tube still in his mouth. He reached up to feel the tube in his mouth. "Let me get a nurse," I said pressing the Nurse's call button on the remote for the bed.

"Yes," a nurse entered quickly.

"He's awake," I pointed to Marcus. "Can we get that tube out his mouth?"

"Oh thank goodness. Yes let me let the doctor know," she said leaving as quickly as he arrived.

• • • •

WITHIN 15 - 20 MINUTES, they had removed the breathing tube and turned off the machine that had been keeping him alive. He looked groggy and in pain but he was alive. He was drowsy from the medication they were pumping him while he was sleeping.

"Nigga, you got some timing," I said looking at him.

• • • •

"I HEARD YOU," HE WHISPERED, trying to get his voice back. "I heard you talking to me,"

• • • •

"YOU HEARD ME? FOR REAL?"

• • • •

"YEP, I HEARD YOU SAY you wanted me to *wake the fuck up*," he stammered.. That shit in the movie was real. That shit worked. Marcus heard me talking to him.

"Damn man, I'm glad to have you back," I grinned, giving him a handshake and a pound.

"Glad to be back," he said, closing his eyes and tears streaming down his face. "Where's Siedah dawg?"

"She here still,"

"Is she okay?"

"Yeah, she got hit in the chest like you did,"

"Did they find out who did it?" he asked. I didn't want to tell him but I needed to.

"Yeah, it was the nigga that was following Siedah,"

Marcus' eyes widened. "Really? Where did they catch him?"

"He killed himself. He was found not far from y'all," I responded.

He was shocked. "Are you fucking serious?" he struggled to get louder and grabbed his throat.

"I wish I was fucking around, but yes, I'm serious," I said handing him some water with the *hospital ice*.

"Glad that motherfucker is gone," he said before taking a sip. "He never deserved Siedah,"

"He didn't deserve anyone," I said. Marcus shook his head in agreement.

"How is she? How is Siedah?" he asked. I smiled at him as I could do one better than answering him.

"Let me go and get her and you can find out for yourself," I said.

"Really?" he said, sounding excited. He was ready to see Siedah. He really loved her.

"Yeah. See I knew you were in love," I joked. He rolled his eyes and pointed towards the door.

"Nigga go and get my baby. I need to see her," he said.

"Now you demanding?" I loved fucking with him. I'm grateful that he's still here for me to do so. "I'll be back, hold on." I said leaving the room and heading to get Siedah.

• • • •

SIEDAH

• • • •

FRANKLIN CAME BACK in just the right time as my family had left to go celebrate. They came early to see me because they wouldn't be able to do so later.

"Oh good, you came back at the right time, my family just left," I said as I sat on the side of the bed.

"Oh ok cool," he said walking into the room. "I'm gonna need you to put your robe so I can take you for a stroll,"

"Oooo yeah, I haven't been out of the room all day," I said, grabbing my robe and my fluid monitor and we were on our way.

We had walked for a while before I realized we had left the area and we were heading towards the ICU. I suddenly got nervous and my stomach twisted in knots. I stopped as I felt overwhelmed.

"What's going on?" Franklin asked as I stopped in the hallway.

"What if he's mad at me?" I asked.

"Mad? Why would he be mad?" he asked. He sounded like Monica.

"Because of what happened," I said. I was scared he was mad.

"Girl, he knows that wasn't your fault. That nigga that followed you was crazy," he said

"But, Marcus got shot because of me,"

"You got shot too." He speaks the truth.

I did get shot.

Hell, I got shot *first*.

• • • •

WE WALKED INTO THE ICU unit and walked over to Marcus's room. I was nervous as I stood at the door. I looked at Franklin and he nodded for me to go in. He pushed and held the door open so I could come in.

I saw Marcus laying in the bed. The nurses were working on him, checking his vitals and asking if he was in pain. When he saw me, his face lit up. He was surprised to see me standing at the door. Tears started falling as I watched him gaze at me while nurses checked everything before they left.

He watched me as they left and I slowly walked over to the side of the bed. He looked at me, his face was turning red as tears started streaming down his cheeks.

"Baby girl," he said as he reached for me. I burst out crying as he still wanted me. I was still his *baby girl*. I grabbed his hand and he pulled me closer to him.

"Baby," I said as I leaned closer to him. If I could be in the bed with him, I would've. I wrapped my arms around him, reaching carefully through the series of tubes. He wrapped his arms around me and grunted as he tried to hold me tight.

"I missed you so much, baby girl," he whispered in my ear as he continued to hold me.

"I missed you too baby, I'm so sorry," I said as I cried harder. "I'm sorry baby....I'm...I'm..,"

"Baby girl, it's okay. It's not your fault," he said as I raised up to see his face. I missed the way he looked at me; his eyes just made me melt. "I'm sorry, I should have taken the situation more seriously than I did,"

"I didn't know he would do this, I'm sorry baby, I didn't want you to get hurt,"

"It's okay baby, for real. I'm still here and you are too. I don't think I wouldn't be able to handle it if you didn't make it," he said. I sat on the side of the bed facing him. He lifted his hand and caressed my face. I touched and held the back of his hand.

"I thought I had lost you," I said looking down, holding his hand. I laced my fingers with his. He kissed the back of my hand and smiled.

"I'm still here, baby girl. I'm not going anywhere," he said, holding both of my hands, smiling at me.

"So it looks like I beat you in the crazy ex department," I said jokingly.

"That you did," he said, raising his eyebrows and smiling. "You take the prize for that,"

"That's not the best award to be honest," I said. I wish I didn't win it.

"Well, I got another prize for you," he gazed at me. He looked lovingly at me as he held my hands.

"What?"

"My heart," he said. My heart flipped and butterflies filled my stomach. "I love you Siedah," he confessed looking at me, eyes wide open and no hesitation.

His words resonate in my ears. He loves me. I was afraid of the word but he makes me want to embrace it. I want to embrace it fully with him.

"I love you too Marcus," I admitted. A big ass kool-aid smile spread across his face. I leaned down and kissed him softly. I missed his lips. I missed kissing him. I missed the way he held me when he kissed me as he cupped my neck. I loved him so much.

"I've been waitin' for you to say those word to me,"

"You've been waiting for me? You know you fell in love with me the minute you met me," I said as I gave him a quick kiss.

"Nah, you fell in love with me first," he said, poking me in the side. "It was my skills,"

"Let's just say it just happened," I said.

"Agreed," he smiled.

"I'm glad you woke up on New Years,"

"Why?"

"So we can start the New Year together,"

"Yeah, we got nowhere to go but up from here, baby girl,"

"True,"

"Happy New Year baby girl, I love you," Marcus said again. My ears danced hearing him tell me he loved me.

"Happy New Year baby, I love you too," I said, giving him a soft, deep kiss.

I had Marcus back with me. I was happy.

Really happy. *And in Love.*

Chapter 13 - Valentine's Day

SIEDAH

• • • •

NEW YEAR'S DAY WAS a good day. Marcus and I got a chance to share it together, even though we were both in the hospital. I got my walking papers about a week before he did, as they wanted to make sure everything was good before they released Marcus due to him being in a coma for a week.

Of course I was there to pick Marcus when he finally got released. That was the happiest of all days. Seeing him dressed in a pair of baggy jeans, a hoodie and his big ass winter coat, was a welcoming sight from the hospital gown.

"Ready to go?" I said holding on to the wheelchair to escort him out.

"Hell yeah, I'm ready to go. You shouldn't have to push me though,"

"Well, you gotta be in the wheelchair to leave the hospital, so sit yo' ass down," I said pointing to the chair. He shook his head and sat down.

"You lucky I love you," he said laughing as I pushed him out into the hallway.

'Naw, you're the lucky one," I replied.

"Yes I am."

I drove to Marcus' studio and a person could tell we hadn't been there in a while. Our Christmas gifts were on the couch. Franklin said that the police had gathered and given him all the gifts that had fallen out of the truck. Franklin just placed them on the couch and placed all the flowers we got in the hospital on any surface throughout the studio. The decorations were still up and glowing. I remembered us being in the bed just before we left to go to the party. It seemed like so long ago and not 2-3 weeks. As soon as I got Marcus settled, my phone started ringing - it was Monica.

"Hello?"

"Hey Bitch, you and Marcus home?"

"Yeah, we just got here, wassup?"

"Franklin and I wanted to come by and see y'all and see if y'all need anything,"

"Oh ok, why don't y'all stop and get some food from Lawrence Fisheries, we haven't eaten yet," I asked.

"Oh ok cool, we'll do that. See you in a minute," she said, hanging up the phone.

"Monica and Franklin are coming over and they are bringing food,"

"Oh ok," he said, coming over to me. He grinned and smoothed a few locs back behind my ears. "I'm so happy to be back home with you," he pulled me into his embrace.

"Me too, I don't know what I would have done if I lost you," I mumbled as I nuzzled my face under his chin and against his neck.

"I know I would be lost if I had lost you," he said, caressing my back. He held me tight and I didn't want to leave his embrace. "I love you baby girl," he said, planting a kiss on my cheek.

"I love you too," I didn't have to hesitate on how I felt about Marcus.

I was sure I loved him. I was lost when I thought I lost him. I had never had that feeling in my entire life. I felt as though my heart was being pulled out of my chest.

He was my heart.

Marcus

· · · ·

THINGS WERE FINALLY getting back to normal. Franklin and I were finally getting the recognition we deserved. We won the Grammy for the song we produced and that just opened more opportunities for me and Franklin. Our company was growing and we were making a name for ourselves in the music industry.

Siedah was with me and I was happy. All that shit we went through and she was still there for me, I knew she was the one. I guess it would take something tragic to make a person realize that we need to be thankful for those who are in our lives when they are there and appreciate them everyday. And to tell them you love them because tomorrow is not promised. Just as I thought things had quieted down, things took a turn. Not for the worst, just unexpected.

· · · ·

"HELLO?" I ANSWERED the phone as I was working trying to put a track together.

· · · ·

"YES, MAY I SPEAK TO Mr. Marcus Harper?" The male voice said on the other side.

· · · ·

"SPEAKING, HOW CAN I help you?"

· · · ·

"MR. HARPER, THIS IS Officer Daniels of the Chicago Police Department. We wanted to contact you that we have some new evidence that we may need your assistance," he said.

• • • •

"EVIDENCE? WHAT DO YOU mean? The motherfucker that shot me and my girl is dead,"

• • • •

"YES SIR, DUE TO THE holidays our team was backed up and on vacation to get the ballistics pushed through for the case,"

• • • •

"OKAY, SO WHAT DOES that mean?"

• • • •

"WHAT THAT MEANS IS that the same gun that shot you and your girlfriend is not the same gun that killed Mr. Greene," Officer Daniels stated.

"So he *didn't* kill himself?" I asked. *Ain't that some shit*, I thought.

"No, he did not," he replied. "Do you have any cameras on your building Sir? If you do, they may have captured the killer,"

• • • •

"YEAH I DO,"

• • • •

"OK, I'LL COME OVER and get a copy of your recording from that day if you don't mind,"

• • • • •

"NO, I DON'T MIND AT all," I said, hanging up the phone.

Just as I was about to call Siedah, she walked in the door.

"Hey baby," she said as she stomped the snow off of her feet. She smiled as she took off her coat and walked over to me.

"Hey baby girl," I stood up and wrapped my arms around her. It felt so good having her in my arms.

"How's it going?" she said as she backed up to take off her boots.

"It's going good, I'm about to add your part to it," I answered. Siedah helped me on a track and sang for me. She has an amazing voice. I can see us doing a lot of work together in the future. We can build this shit together. She's a good woman to have by my side.

• • • •

"REALLY? I WANNA HEAR it," she said sitting next to me at the soundboard.

"Oh guess what? I got a call from the CPD,"

"For what?" she said looking confused.

• • • •

"THEY SAID THAT GERALD was shot by someone else. That he didn't kill himself,"

"You fucking lying!" she said, widening her eyes.

• • • •

"NOPE, THEY WANT ME to get my security footage from that night. They're sending someone to pick up a copy."

• • • •

"WOW, WHO COULD HAVE shot him?"

"Shit, I was about to ask you the same thing." I said. "He may have had an obsessed stalker too,"

"Shit, he could have. That's some strange shit. So did you look at the footage?"

• • • •

"NAW NOT YET, I WAS just about to go back to that day," I said, sliding to one side of my desk to access my computer.

"I don't know if I want to see it," she said. I completely understand. I didn't want to see the moment we were almost extracted from this world.

"I feel you baby girl," I said looking at her. She rolled her chair over to me and laid her head on my shoulder as we watched the video together.

We watched as we pulled up and took a moment in the truck. We laughed as we saw the camera flash from inside the truck. Siedah had taken a picture when we had just arrived. I was excited about her staying over and she wanted a picture.

I saw myself get out of the suv and walked around to the other side. Unfortunately, we were on the other side of the vehicle so the camera could only view the tops of our heads. Then it happened. I saw a tall figure walking across the street.

It was Gerald. He had parked in front of the studio before we arrived, that's why we didn't hear any cars driving down the street that night. I see him shoot Siedah. I shook my head as tears started flowing down my face. I remember her screaming from that night. It made my blood run cold just thinking about it.

I sniffed as I wiped tears away. Siedah was crying too as she saw Gerald shoot me and fall to the ground. Then just as Gerald was walking over to finish us off, someone quickly walked up from what seemed like the opposite side of the street and shot Gerald square in the head.

As he fell to the ground, they hesitated and then looked directly at the camera. I zoomed and focused in on the person and we were fucking floored - *it was Justine!*

"That's Justine!" Siedah said, covering her mouth.

"Yes the fuck it was," I said. I didn't know how to process what I had just seen. Justine killed Gerald and walked away. Like nothing happened. I wondered if she had that shit planned.

"Oh my goodness, what are you going to do?" she asked.

"I don't know, what do you think we should do?"

"I don't want to turn her in, she has a kid," she begged. I completely understand what she was saying. The kid didn't deserve to be away from his mother because she did something stupid. However it saved us, but stupid as fuck.

"Why do you think she did it?" I asked.

"Maybe she was protecting you," she responded. Maybe she was. "Even though she's not with you anymore, she still cares for you. You two have a history together, that's not just going to go away," Siedah said.

Justine and I had a lot of history together. Over 10 years of ups and downs. She had a moment of weakness that messed it all up. And she has to live with the consequences.

"Yeah, maybe she was. It don't make it right though, but I feel you," I answered.

"She has a kid, baby," Siedah said. I could have sworn Justine had grown on her as if she was pleading her case. "Can you erase just a bit? Just the part when she looks into the camera,"

• • • •

I LOOKED AT HER WITH her eyes so big, beautiful and brown. She was begging me to spare her. Justine helped us in more ways than one. She took out Gerald and simply disappeared.

"Yeah I can, for you baby," I said, giving her a small kiss on the tip of her nose. Her eyes sparkled as she smiled. I made a copy of the video and deleted Justine looking at the camera on the copy for the police. I kept the original, which I wasn't going to delete. I wanted to keep it just in case, that's just me.

• • • •

WE HANDED THE VIDEO over to the police and they said they will reach out to us when they have any leads. We knew they wouldn't because no one knew it was Justine until she looked at the camera. She was out of our lives and we were moving on.

• • • •

VALENTINE'S DAY WAS finally here and I was looking forward to it. Franklin and Monica planned a Valentine's Day dinner and invited a few close friends. The party was our first outing since the incident so when we arrived everybody was happy to see us. We were hugging everyone as they were glad we made it through.

"Hey Dawg," Franklin said as he saw me. "It's good to have you back in action nigga," he gave me a bro hug and handshake.

"It's good to be back for real,"

"And you with Siedah too," he smiled. I closed my eyes and shook my head.

"Yes we are together," I said, looking at her across the room talking to Monica.

"I know nigga, I knew it was gonna happen," he quipped.

"Yeah, she's the real deal Brah," I said smiling at her. She smiled back as she blushed. I loved that woman.

We had a great time at dinner laughing and talking with good friends. Monica and Franklin had a house full of people as I looked around. It was full of people we loved and cared about and whom we called *family*.

I stood up to get everyone's attention, "Excuse me everyone," I said standing up at the table. Everyone looked towards me and quieted down. I suddenly got nervous with all the eyes but I needed to make a statement.

• • • •

"FIRST I WANT TO THANK God for allowing ALL of us to be here right now," I began. "Because a few weeks ago, Siedah and I almost didn't make it,"

"Amen!" Monica said.

"Yes Lord,"

"Ain't God good?"

"All The Time," A few people said in unison.

"Second, I want to Thank All of you who sent Siedah and I prayers and well wishes for a speedy recovery,"

"Good to have y'all back," Someone yelled and we laughed.

"Third, I want to thank my best friends. My brother for life, Franklin, and his beautiful partner Monica for always being there when we needed y'all,"

"Oh shit Marcus!" Monica said as she was wiping away tears. "Why did you hafta do this to me?" she said. Everybody giggled.

"I just want to say I love you guys, we wouldn't be here if it weren't for you coming and supporting us," I said. Everyone clapped and cheered.

"And lastly," I said, getting a lump in my throat. I turned to Siedah, who was sitting next to me and had no idea what I was about to say. She looked at me like a deer in headlights, her eyes as wide as they could be.

"Siedah," I said, holding her hands. Monica's eyes widened and she covered her mouth. "You have been there for me since the day I met you," she looked at me as tears started flowing down her face.

"You were down with everything I was dealing with and you handled it like a real woman should. You had my back through it all. You stuck with me during all of this bullshit, even when you had your own bullshit to deal with and I want to say thank you and I love you, " I said looking at her. She shook her head in approval.

"It's okay baby, I got you. I love you too," she said.

"And I wanted to ask you," I said, pulling a ring box out of my pocket. Everybody started getting excited and loud. Monica and Franklin were standing up to get a better view.

I kneeled down on one knee in front of Siedah and opened the ring box to reveal a 4 carat, 3 Pear shaped Diamond ring. Siedah covered her mouth in amazement.

"Siedah, will you marry me?" I asked. I was nervous as fuck but I only wanted one answer. Siedah looked at me and started crying.

"Yes!" she said, shaking her head in agreement. She held out her hand and I slipped it on her finger.

Perfect fit.

I stood up and wrapped my arms tightly around her. I spun her around as she held onto me tightly. Everybody cheered as I was overjoyed. I looked at Siedah and kissed her deeply in front of everyone.

"To the Room!" Monica yelled and we all laughed.

Monica walked over to congratulate us, as did everyone else. Siedah was happy as she was showing off the ring. Franklin came over and shook my hand.

"Nigga!" he said, giving me a hug. "Dude, I knew it, I just knew it,"

"You ain't know shit," I said.

"I had a feeling then," he said. We laughed. He handed me a beer and we toasted to a beautiful life.

I was looking forward to a beautiful life, with a beautiful and amazing woman.

That's why I love her.

· · · ·

MARCUS

· · · ·

SIEDAH AND I WAITED until everyone else had left, when we decided to tell Franklin and Monica about what we saw on the security video.

"Hey we got something to tell y'all," I said as we sat in the living room relaxing.

"Wassup?" Franklin said as he rolled a blunt.

"The police called us the other day and said that the gun that was used to shoot us was not the same gun that shot Gerald,"

"What the fuck?" Franklin said.

"What, he didn't shoot himself?" Monica asked.

"Nope, he didn't," Siedah answered.

"Whaaaaaat?" Monica sang.

"Then who killed him?" Franklin asked.

"We looked at the security video because the cops want the footage to see if they could see who else was there,"

"Did y'all see someone?" Franklin asked as he lit the end of the blunt.

"Yeah," I replied.

"Who was it?" Monica asked. I looked at Siedah and she looked at me and raised her eyebrows to go on.

"Justine."

"SHUT THE FUCK UP!" Monica yelled. Franklin damn near choked on the smoke.

"Yup,"

"Are you fucking serious man?" he said.

"Well what are y'all gonna do? Are you gonna give the copy to the police?" Monica asked.

"Yeah we are gonna give them a copy,"

"She got a kid too man," Monica said, shaking her head.

"That's what we said too," Siedah said. "That's why we decided to delete that part from the copy,"

"Oh thank goodness," Monica said, holding her chest. "I know what she did to you Marcus was wrong but she don't deserve the consequences from this,"

"Right, we thought the same way," I said.

"Isn't she gone anyway?" Franklin said as he passed the blunt to Monica.

"Yeah, she left the day of the party,"

"The day we got shot," Siedah said.

"Wow, that's some shit," Franklin said. "She saved y'all lives,"

"Yup she did." I said.

Justine saved our lives. Even though she went a little crazy for a moment, in the end she saved our lives.

Siedah told me that she had run into Justine one night when she was leaving the studio and she told me what she said to Justine. I guess it resonated with her because she disappeared after that. I wanted the best for her, even though we were no longer together. I'm glad she came to her senses when she did. Or that could have just been Siedah being the real woman she was and standing up for her man.

We never heard from Justine again and we were fine with that. The police eventually said the case was unsolved due to no witnesses and nothing to lead them to Gerald's killer. Siedah and I were happy it was finally over and we could move on with our lives. We decided to move in together since we got engaged. We weren't rushing anything either as we haven't set a date. It will eventually happen, but we were going to take one day at a time just like we did with our relationship.

We were focused on enjoying being together.

www.ingramcontent.com/pod-product-compliance
Lightning Source LLC
Chambersburg PA
CBHW022136150726
47992CB00002B/619